Her Hair in

Fiery Points

Tales from the Angels' Share
Volume 3

Marella Sands

Word Posse

Dedication
To everyone who's agreed to be on my YouTube channel.
Couldn't do it without you!

The Angels' Share Books
Volume 1: Through a Keyhole, Darkly
Volume 2: What the Thunder Said
Volume 3: The Chair She Sat In
Volume 4: With Sleepless Eye
Volume 5: Past the Isle of Dogs
Volume 6: When We Had Feathers
Volume 7: Feeding the Bird of Tondal
Volume 8: A Heap of Broken Images
Volume 9: Her Hair in Fiery Points

Other Word Posse Books by Marella Sands
Pandora's Mirror
Fortune's Daughter
Restless Bones

A New Confederacy Books
Perdition
Purgatory
Perfection
Paradise
Promised Land

Catch up with the author on various platforms:
www.MarellaSands.com
Facebook: facebook.com/MarellaSands
YouTube: @marellasands6260

ISBN-13: 978-1-944089-36-8

1

A giant flamingo stood above me in the Tampa Airport.

"That is something else," said Brooklyn, my traveling partner. "Do you think we'll see any real flamingoes?"

I glanced up at the huge sculpture. It was only part of a flamingo. The whole effect was that passengers moving through the terminal were walking on the bottom of the pond while two legs, and a head and neck, came down from a rippled glass surface above.

"I don't know," I said. I wasn't sure I liked the sculpture but it did seem kind of nice that it was in an airport. I did not equate *airport* with *public art display*. Maybe I hadn't been to enough airports.

"I saw a documentary on them once," said Brooklyn as we headed down an escalator toward the baggage claim area. "Did you know their pink color comes from the shrimp they eat?"

"Huh," I said. I hadn't known that and didn't really care to know it now. But Brooklyn was trying to keep me engaged in what was going on around me. Staying interested and present in my own life was becoming harder and harder. I had reached out to her once the remoteness I felt toward everything around me began to frighten me. It should have been even more frightening that my fear was slowly draining away, when it should by rights it should continue to escalate.

Brooklyn had walked on ahead looking for the correct carousel. The airport didn't have an overwhelming number; I was sure we would find our luggage easily enough.

Brooklyn's hair, which was usually green or blue or some other wild color, was black now. This time, the fashion statement was coming from her clothing: her jacket consisted of a riot of reds, greens, blues, and purples. On top of that, on the back, was a peace symbol in sequins, so she reflected the light like some kind of latter-day Disco queen.

I'd let Brooklyn make all the arrangements; she was not shy about spending someone else's money, and I had what amounted to an unlimited spending account. At least, Ware, my old boss at The Angels' Share, had never said anything about limits and there had never been threats to cut me off, no matter how much of Ware's money I allowed Brooklyn to spend.

Money meant nothing to me now. I'd never had much, but with all the insanity in my life, even the concept of money had been losing any kind of importance. I could find myself going days without eating or even thinking about going to get food, either at the grocery store or a restaurant. The hotel room I'd been living in for three months was being paid for by Ware, so I had had little to do except sit on the bed and look out the window.

Brooklyn had already spotted our bags. She hauled her bright pink bag off the belt and pointed me toward my small black bag. A neon green handkerchief was tied around the handle, which immediately made it apparent which bag was mine in a veritable *ocean* of small black bags.

Once we had our bags, we stepped outside into the warm salt-laden air. The palm trees and strange flowered bushes were alien to my midwestern sensibilities.

I let Brooklyn take care of picking up the rental car and merely climbed into the passenger seat when we were ready to go. "Here," she said as she handed me a paper road map. "We can begin marking off places we've checked for this sinkhole you're looking for. Or, we can begin after checking in to the hotel and getting some lunch."

I looked at the map incredulously. "They still make the paper version of these things?"

"Obviously. You know how to read one, don't you?"

"Seriously? It's a paper map, not Einstein's equations."

Brooklyn laughed. "Well, I know Andre can't use one. When I handed him this one, he had it *upside down*. You'd think the fact that the labels were unreadable would have been a clue."

Andre was Brooklyn's cousin. My late partner, Castro, had been friends with Andre, which is how we had originally met Brooklyn. Now Castro was gone.

I'd killed him.

I hadn't known I was doing it, but I'd done it. That fact had torn me up for months. Now the thought barely had the power to upset me.

That wasn't normal.

But then, what in my life had been normal for several years now? My boss and his compatriots had turned out to be supernatural creatures who had once roamed through galaxies fighting among themselves and destroying anything that got in their way, including the very stars themselves.

Brooklyn had piloted the car onto a long causeway that crossed a large body of water.

"Tampa Bay," said Brooklyn. "At least, that's Tampa in the rear view mirror."

"Where are we going?"

"Ooh, a question," she said. "She shows some curiosity."

"Enjoy it while it lasts."

"I will," she said. She tried to sound lighthearted but the sadness was evident in her voice. She had been trying so hard to get me to care about anything, but so far she'd been unsuccessful. It wasn't her fault life no longer held any interest or meaning for me. Castro was dead. My boss and his stupid fellow supernatural shits continued to plague my very existence. Nothing in my life seemed to be under my control or even my influence anymore.

Not even this trip. About a month ago, I'd started dreaming of a place near the sea. I'd seen the palm trees, the white beaches, the shells scattered over the beach. The dream sometimes continued to the point where I had managed to spot a few landmarks. House numbers, street signs, stuff like that. I hadn't put too much importance on it, but one day when Brooklyn had come by for her occasional "wellness check," I'd mentioned the dream.

That was when she had suddenly decided we needed to go find this place. The next night the dream had been even more memorable, showing me a stadium. It hadn't taken Brooklyn five minutes to Google enough stadium pictures to show me that what I was seeing was located in St. Petersburg, Florida. Apparently, some sports teams played there; I didn't know which ones and didn't care.

When Brooklyn mentioned flying down to look around St. Petersburg for whatever the dream wanted me to find, the dream had stopped coming. The two of us were taking that to mean that, once we were planning to act, the dream had done what it needed to do. We were supposed to come here.

Whether or not that was a good thing or a bad thing was unknown. Not that I cared at the moment, anyway.

Brooklyn hummed to herself quietly and pulled into a hotel parking lot. We checked in and Brooklyn tossed our bags in the room. "Okay, I'm starved. Lunch, and then we start our quest."

I let her pick the place. She chose a small taco place a couple of blocks away from the hotel. The tacos were acceptable in quality despite the fact it seemed odd to eat tacos in Florida. Shouldn't we be eating fish, or crab legs, or something?

"Any ideas where we should start?" she asked as we got back in the car and let the air conditioning flow over our bodies. The day wasn't terribly hot, but it was certainly much warmer than the weather back in St. Louis. Why did people live here voluntarily?

Who'd want to be sweaty all year round?

"Teryl?"

"Yeah."

"Any idea of where to start?"

I took a deep breath and glanced at the map. Nothing seemed particularly interesting on it.

Brooklyn leaned over. "The botanical garden is just a few blocks from here. Why not start there?"

"Is there a reason for that? I mean, a botanical garden?"

"Well, it won't be in the same class as Shaw's Garden," said Brooklyn. "But I remember something on the website saying it had a low point that's in a sinkhole. A real-world physical one, not a magical one. Why not check a sinkhole for a sinkhole?"

"Sure."

It didn't take long for Brooklyn to get us to a parking lot next to an area that was clearly full of a variety of trees. Yep. Botanical garden.

I got out of the car, but a movement toward the street caught my eye. A woman, staring at us.

I tried not to show I had noticed that her attention was on Brooklyn and myself. She was rather short, somewhat plump, and dressed in a light blue blouse paired with beige pants. She looked neat and classy, fairly unremarkable, actually, except for the intensity of her gaze.

I followed Brooklyn into the building where she purchased our tickets. We exited into the garden itself; only a wrought iron fence separated us from the parking lot. I glanced around, but the woman had left...except I noticed her in the building speaking to the person who had sold us the entrance tickets.

Clearly, she was following us. But how could she have known we'd come here? It was as if she had been waiting for someone to shadow.

Maybe she was just crazy and had picked us randomly, but that seemed like quite a stretch of believability.

"We're being followed," I said softly to Brooklyn. Her eyes widened slightly, but she was pretty good at keeping her reactions to herself.

"Who?"

"Woman wearing beige pants currently buying an entrance ticket."

Brooklyn frowned. She glanced around slowly, pretending to be interested in the small pond nearby, but snuck a glance at the building. "I thought I saw a woman like that at the baggage carousel in the airport."

"So she's managed to follow us to the hotel, to lunch, and now here. Great."

"What do we do?" Brooklyn didn't seem uneasy; she'd seen much weirder and more alarming things since meeting me. A plump woman following us wasn't going to get her worked up, not until and unless we learned something about the woman that clued us in to how dangerous she might be.

I pointed toward a large tree. "Let's stand on the other side, and when she comes by, we ask her what the hell is going on."

"Sounds good to me," said Brooklyn.

We got behind the tree and waited. It was only a couple minutes before we saw the woman hurry on by. She seemed slightly worried, as if losing track of us while paying the entry fee was a terrible thing.

I stepped out into the sun and said, "Hey, you! Why are you following us?"

The woman jumped in surprised and spun around. Her mouth hung open. I'd managed to surprise her, at least.

"I, uh..."

"If you're trying to think up a lie, don't bother. I can usually tell when someone's lying." Actually, I couldn't do anything like that, but I didn't mind lying about it if it would get me more information.

"You were at the airport, now you're here," said Brooklyn. She sounded angry. "If nothing else, that's just rude."

I almost laughed at the ridiculousness of that statement.

The woman stepped back and blinked several times. She still seemed to be recovering from the shock of us catching her out.

"Well?" I asked after giving her a few seconds to pull herself together.

"I'm here to keep an eye on you, yes," she said. "Because you're in terrible danger."

"Tell me something I don't know."

"Danger's our middle name," said Brooklyn, almost at the same time.

The woman's mouth twitched and her eyes narrowed. We were not making a good impression on her, though why I should want to, or care to, I didn't know.

"Who is it?" I asked. "Garnett? Marveaux? Mink? Lucy?" I named the supernatural shits who annoyed me the most.

"Worse," she said. "Me."

2

"Okay," I said. "And who are you?"

"Madrigal Evers," she said. She paused, one eyebrow raised.

I realized she was waiting for one, or both, of us to have some kind of reaction.

"Never heard of you," I said after a few tense moments. "You sure you got the right bartender?"

She visibly deflated slightly, and her expression grew even more cross. "Ware didn't tell you."

Brooklyn let out an exaggerated sigh. "Well, obviously not. But stop speaking in riddles and tell us outright what you want us to know, and then let us look at this pretty garden for a while. Unmolested, unaccompanied, you know?"

The woman opened her mouth, then closed it. I was tempted to tell her to stop acting like a fish gulping air, but decided against it. She needed to be the one talking, not me.

"I was a bartender for Ware years ago," she said. "It didn't take me long to realize something odd was going on at that bar. Like that thing he has roaming around his office. The weird friends who show up to drink but who never age. Strange visitors who make your skin crawl."

"Yeah, sure," I said. "Why does that make you dangerous?"

"I have information. You don't really know who you're working for."

I laughed at that. The sudden burst of mirth felt good. I couldn't remember the last time I'd laughed.

"Ms. Evers," said Brooklyn. "I don't think you know half the stuff we've witnessed and suffered in the past couple of years. So, of proclaiming yourself to be more dangerous than Marveaux is what gets you up in the morning, fine. But we have a botanical garden to walk through."

"It's Riga," she said. "Not Ms. Evers."

That had to be about the last thing I'd expected. Here she tried to be so threatening, then tossed out her nickname like we were going to be pals?

"At least you aren't Maddie or Gaga," Brooklyn said. "No dignity there. No offense to anyone named Maddie or Gaga, I suppose."

Riga's nostrils flared, which was fascinating as I was pretty sure I thought that only happened in movies or books. I got the suspicion we were nothing like she had assumed we would be. More mouthy, surely.

"You have no idea of the dangers you face," she said.

Before Brooklyn could say anything, I laughed and said, "Look, if you want to continue to try to be threatening, I guess you can, but we're moving along now. Trying to scare us with statements like *you have no idea of the dangers you face* isn't going to cut it. I killed a Rake with my bare hands a few months ago. Hell, I *killed my own boyfriend*. You posturing about being dangerous isn't earning you any points from me. You look like a somewhat tanned Mrs. Marple. Or maybe Jessica Fletcher. In any case, I don't give a shit what you think, what you threaten, or your self-image. Have a mai tai and sit in a chaise on a beach. I've got shit to do."

I turned away and walked around a few tall palm trees, moving along the concrete path that took me past quite a few plants I recognized from the garden area at Home Depot. Crotons and mother-in-law tongues. Sheffleria and Dracaena. Money trees and rubber plants. Here they grew outside of pots, no doubt happy to have a warm climate and all the sandy soil they could ask for. I'd always felt a bit sad for the small pot-bound tropical plants back home, having to live in tiny clay or plastic containers in dark drafty homes where the winter air was dry and the summer air heavy and wet until the air conditioners were turned on and the air became cold and dry. Winter year-round, at least as far as the tropical plants were concerned.

If plants could be happy, I bet these were. I was jealous.

The path went up a short slope and broke out into a small open lawn surrounded by bougainvillea and pitcher plant vines.

"Bet they have weddings here," said Brooklyn. "I couldn't imagine a prettier spot."

"Maybe so," I said, my heart clenching at the word *wedding* even though Castro and I had never talked about making our partnership official with signed documents and whatever else went with getting married. "Aren't we looking for a sinkhole?"

"Oh yeah," said Brooklyn. "I guess Ms. Evers...*Riga*...can you believe that name?...distracted me." She glanced at the map of the garden she had from the front desk. "It's in that direction." She waved the map at another path which entered the clearing on the same side as the first, but closer to a small garden of flowers I couldn't identify.

"There's something called the Growing Stone located at the lowest spot in the garden. It's fifteen feet below street level. That's the current bottom of the sinkhole. Supposedly if you sit on the stone, you'll be given tranquility and inner harmony."

"Then I guess we'd better go there immediately," I said. "I could certainly use some inner harmony."

The stone itself was easy to find. Brooklyn actually clapped her hands in glee when she saw it. "It looks like a stromatolite!" she exclaimed.

I looked at her blankly. Yes, I could tell a mother-in-law's tongue from a rubber plant, but that was mostly due to Castro's habit of watching a lot of gardening shows on TV. He never watched shows on rocks.

"What's a stroma, strooma..."

"Stromatolite. They were the some of the first colonial organisms on the planet. Probably our billions of generations ago ancestors. They were some of the first who learned how to convert carbon dioxide and sunlight into fuel and oxygen. The oxygen combined with iron in the ancient oceans and the stromatolites literally *rusted the entire planet*. Isn't that cool?"

"Trippy," I said. "Rusting a planet. Respect."

"Yeah," said Brooklyn happily. "That's on my bucket list: to see some of the banded iron formations that were laid down then. Can you imagine? Hundreds of feet of sediment made up largely of rust."

I was rapidly losing interest. "Yeah," I said. "Sure. Lots of rusty rocks."

Brooklyn gave me a smile, "I know it's not so intriguing to you, Teryl. But it's good to see you at least showing a tiny bit of interest in the world around you. Just a small bit. That was all I was hoping for when we decided to come here."

"Goals."

"Yep. Goals. Now, go sit on the rock. Get yourself some inner tranquility or whatever."

I sighed and sat down on the rock. Others were wandering by, giving us long looks. They probably wanted to sit, too. So I popped back up. "If you're going to sit, sit. Then let's move along. There are others waiting."

"Oh, I'm fine," said Brooklyn. "Come on. I hear there's some flamingoes here. I'd like to see a real one, and they've got more than one."

"Okay, flamingoes."

Brooklyn consulted her map again and I followed her across a grassy meadow, over a tiny brook full of papyrus, under a ramada sporting several dozen orchids.

"The quick tour," said Brooklyn. "Flamingoes ahead."

I said nothing. She could take a direct route or a roundabout route, whichever she preferred.

"Sensing anything?" she said. "I've been taking us back and forth across this entire sinkhole."

"Hadn't noticed anything."

"Were you even trying?"

I didn't say anything.

"Thought so," said Brooklyn. "At least try."

"I don't know what to do."

Brooklyn waved her arms around helplessly. "You're the one having dreams about finding this sinkhole. So...what do you do in the dreams?"

I'd told her before but clearly she wanted me to go through it again. "I just feel something. Like it's speaking to me in the back of my head. I can simply feel where it is."

The "it" in question was the sinkhole where Ware had stuffed his chief rival and best friend after their war was over and they had retreated to the relative safety of Earth. I suspected I should be able to sense it since I was descended from the greatest of Ware's species, his lover and the woman he'd literally worshipped and followed across a hundred thousand star systems. Zireya.

Zireya had managed to have a child with a human man. I was a descendant of that hybrid child, and it seemed I had inherited a tiny jot of Zireya's power. It was that miniscule bit of power I hoped would show me the way to the mystical pocket universe, the sinkhole, that I sought.

"I don't think what we're looking for is here. But that would be too easy, anyway. A magical sinkhole contained inside a real-world sinkhole?

Brooklyn shook her head. "Okay, flamingoes, then we go. Right?"

"Right."

At last, we came across an enclosure with a small pond. A couple dozen large pink birds stood around, looking both ridiculous and dignified at the same time.

I turned around and there was Riga, just as plump and just as put-out as before. "I hope you've had a good time in the gardens," she said.

"Oh, I have."

"Yeah, it's okay," said Brooklyn. "I mean, St. Louis has one of the premiere botanical gardens in the *world*, so this is nice but nothing like what we've got back home."

"Sure, St. Louis is better," I said. "But what I want to know is, why you are following us around, Riga? So you can try to scare us?"

"Not scare you," she said. "I'm not sure why you're here, but it can't be good if Ware sent you."

"He didn't send me," I said. "I haven't seen him in months."

Riga took a moment to absorb this. "But you're here to try to find Isya's sinkhole."

There seemed no point in denying it. "Uh-huh. I don't know if I'll be calling up Ware to let him know if we find it. But, yeah. I have a vested interest in seeing Earth survive, so I'd rather Ware and Isya not go to war again. Enough destruction was caused the first time."

"Do you know where the sinkhole is?" Brooklyn asked. "You could save us a lot of time."

"No," said Riga. "Nor would I tell you. If you are determined to find it, I'll stop you."

Brooklyn tossed her hair back over her shoulder. "I have a feeling this is the point where one of us says *I'd like to see you try.*"

"I'd like to see you try," I said.

"You should say it with a bit more menace," said Brooklyn.

Once again, we were clearly not reacting the way Riga had thought we would. Her cheeks were red and she clenched her teeth.

"We're going to keep looking," I said. "And you can run to whatever Forlorn you're with, Marveaux or whomever, and try to stop us. Pretty clear what we'll all be doing, yeah?"

Riga's hands had become fists. "You are not taking this seriously."

"Of course I am," I said with some heat of my own. "I told you I take the survival of Earth very seriously. It's *you* I don't take seriously."

"You'll realize that's a mistake soon enough," said Riga.

"Is that a promise?" I asked.

Riga opened her mouth, closed it, and then apparently decided retreat was her best option. She spun on her heels and stalked toward the entrance to the garden.

I watched her go. "Do you think we should start following her now? What do you bet she's lying about knowing where the sinkhole is?"

Brooklyn shrugged. "I have a feeling she'll be around. Let's see what we can do ourselves first, and then let her catch up with us at some point if we think we need help from someone who clearly doesn't want to help."

We left the pink birds, walked by a few more birds in cages, and headed for the exit. Which, of course, made you pass through the gift shop.

"Cute stuff," said Brooklyn as we made our way out of the building. She glanced briefly at a small crystal tchotchke shaped like a lily pad with a frog on it. It was pink and light green and had a small sticker on it that said *I Light Up!*

"You need it?" I asked.

Brooklyn laughed. "Nah. Come on, let's drive around a bit. If you feel anything weird, let me know."

"Fine." Despite the annoyance of Riga following us, I discovered that the whole ridiculousness of the situation had lifted my mood slightly. I paid more attention to what was outside the window. Brooklyn drove the car down wide boulevards lined with flowering crepe myrtle. The flowers ran the gamut of purple to pink to bright white.

It was as if even the very bushes were happy here, unlike everything back home in St. Louis, where hardly anything had bloomed yet and the trees were still bare. The harsh browns and grays of winter remained, even as the days grew longer. But here, everything was green, and what wasn't green was a riot of colors right down to the creamiest off-white I'd ever seen.

If moving to a different city were based on the beauty of its roadside plants, then everyone would move to Florida.

The air was heavy with salt, though I couldn't see the ocean yet. "Did you say we're heading for a beach?"

"Oh, did you finally find something you wanted to do?"

I didn't reply. Brooklyn had been trying to get me to be more active for weeks, but I'd not been cooperative.

"If I thought you'd like Florida, we'd have come earlier," said Brooklyn. "Especially since it would have gotten us out of snow, sleet, and ice country. I always wanted to come here. I had a friend when I was little whose family went to the beach in between every fall and spring semester. She'd come back with stories of Christmases on the beach, and opening presents under the stars while the waves crashed on the shoreline nearby. We always opened presents in the morning, but I guess some people do it on Christmas Eve instead. Don't make the kids wait one more night, right?"

I shrugged. I'd never gotten much of a Christmas. My mother was not only not religious, but she was too busy trying to buy alcohol to worry about presents. Give her two dollars, she would have found a way to buy a shot somewhere, or maybe one of those tiny sample bottles like they distribute on airplanes.

"Well, at least this town is built on a grid system," said Brooklyn. "It may show a certain lack of style, but we can literally drive back and forth from the bay to the gulf while you see what you can sense."

"I don't know that I'll be able to sense anything."

Brooklyn slowed down to stop at a red light. "You keep feeling weird stuff we can't explain. So I think you'll feel *something*. Whether or not you interpret it correctly is another question."

"Thanks."

"Don't mention it. Now, keep your eyes open and your mind...whatever. Open? Receiving? Stretched out? I have no idea what words work for bizarre mind powers."

"Make up some."

Brooklyn gave me a thumbs-up.

I let my mind drift away and merely watched the low buildings and brilliant green foliage go by. Nothing caught my interest.

"Oh, hey, look!" Brooklyn sounded excited.

I glanced up ahead. In the distance I spotted a thin dark blue line.

"That's got to be the Gulf," said Brooklyn. "I know we're here to find Isya's sinkhole, but can we at least go to the beach briefly? I really *really* want to walk on the sand at least once."

"Sure. It's as good a place as any," I said. "Plus, you should have the chance to walk on sand, considering all the time and effort you're putting into taking care of everything." I didn't add, *taking care of me*, though I was grateful for her attention and her tendency to bully me into eating and now, to get away from St. Louis to do something constructive.

The closer we got to the beach, though, the more a sinking feeling began creeping into my gut. I didn't tell Brooklyn to stop, because we were here specifically to find supernatural places or items that only I could sense. This might be it.

The beach was now hidden behind buildings, but I felt it ahead of us. The day might be sunny, but my mood had quickly fallen back into gloom.

3

The beach was prettier than I could have imagined. It was wide and white and the water was aqua and far smoother than any picture of the surf I had ever seen. The place looked more like a giant bathtub than a rough ocean.

Parking hadn't been an issue. Apparently, midday during the work week wasn't people's favorite time to visit. We'd been able to grab a spot right by the walkway to the main beach.

I'd let Brooklyn figure out the electronic payment system and had walked over a small wooden bridge to the fine white sand beyond.

"I love it!" exclaimed Brooklyn. She immediately tossed off her sandals and dug her toes into the sand. "Come on, get rid of your shoes. This is great!"

I did as she bid. The sand was cooler and more abrasive than I had anticipated, but the sensation was not unpleasant.

The two of us walked toward the water. The gently lapping waves made hardly any sound. White birds with ice blue eyes wandered down the beach, giving Brooklyn and me stern glances as they passed. Clearly, they weren't too upset at having to share the area with humans, but would have preferred to have it to themselves.

Brooklyn squealed in delight and reached down to pick up something small and gold. "Look at this seashell!"

"Very pretty," I said. And it was; the thing had bands of brown and white swirling around its exterior while the bit of the interior I could see was a brilliant white.

"There's millions of them!" Brooklyn held onto the shell she had just claimed, but her attention had been snared by the wide band of shells that stretched along the beach as far as one could see.

Far up the beach, I saw two women bending over and picking up things out of the band of shells. I suppose collecting pretty things was a human habit no matter what it might be; rocks, flowers, seashells.

"You could certainly stock a thousand shelves with the booty you'd find here today," I said.

Brooklyn was in ecstasy. "It's so much better than I thought it would be. I'll have to bring a bag next time so I can collect a bunch of shells to take home."

I spotted a shell that had broken lengthwise, exposing the swirls and small compartments of the white interior. I picked it up and inspected it closely. The wet surface was smooth and shone like it had been polished.

"It's broken," said Brooklyn. "A lot of them are."

"I like it," I said. "You can see all the curves and shapes on the inside that you wouldn't see otherwise."

"That's one way to look at it. Let's walk along the beach a bit and you see if you feel anything weird."

"Sure."

The walk was pleasant. We hadn't gotten very far before Brooklyn couldn't contain herself and she jogged toward the surf. She laughed as she splashed the ankle-deep water over her pants.

"You'll be all wet," I said. Nothing like stating the obvious. Maybe I should also announce that it was sunny, that the blue color of the gulf was breathtaking, and that walking along the beach was harder than walking on concrete. The sand shifted under my feet so that every step took a lot more concentration and effort than walking on a stable surface. If I did this enough, I should build up some decent muscles.

I dropped the shell I had picked up; I had no need of things to clutter up my living space, much less a reminder of something that had once been alive and the only evidence of its existence was this broken bit of ephemera.

Brooklyn, on the other hand, had more shells in her hands than she could comfortably hold. Every time she picked up a new one, an old one fell out of her grasp.

I turned back to look at the beach, wondering how far we'd come. I was surprised to see how much ground was had covered; I guess the walk was pleasant enough one could walk and walk without really noticing the distance one had come.

A strange darkness hung over a neighborhood toward an area that was clearly the small shopping district.

"Something's down there," I said.

I was answered only by a few seagulls that glided past and squawked at me angrily as if ordering me off the beach.

I turned around. Brooklyn had continued her way up the beach without noticing I had stopped. She was too entranced by all the shells at her feet.

"Hey!" I shouted. Brooklyn looked around, saw me far behind, and waved. She trotted down to where I was.

"Isn't this great?"

"Yeah," I agreed. "And there's something going on with the town. I can see a kind of dark cloud over something, but we're not close enough for me to tell exactly what it's hovering over."

Brooklyn put a hand up to her brow to shade her eyes. "I don't see any clouds."

"I don't think it's an actual physical cloud," I said. "It's just this...darkness. I don't know what else to call it."

"Okay," said Brooklyn. "Sounds like we have our first clue. Let's go see what darkness haunts this delightfully sunny and beautiful place."

She glanced at all the shells in her hands, sighed and dropped them. "If we come back, I'll have a sack," she said. "But in the meantime, saving the world is more important."

"Naturally," I said. "Let's go save the world."

The two of us walked toward the main area of town. Every step was harder and harder for me to take. It was as if I were a magnet being repelled by the same pole of a second magnet.

But I was no magnet. That was just imagination. I was a person who was caught up in affairs I had no business being a part of. Walking toward something unsettling, if not downright alarming, was one of those things I shouldn't have to do.

And yet, here I was. I continued to walk toward something that did not want me to come any closer.

I didn't like that thought.

4

I stared at the small stone building that sported a sign saying Gulf Beaches Historical Museum.

"This is it," I said. "Whatever darkness is around here is inside this building."

"Huh. I still can't sense anything, but then, that's why you're here. You're the one getting all the attention from Queen Bitch."

"Lucky me."

Queen Bitch was my distant ancestress, an alien from the stars, who had led the remnant of her people to this planet. Under her direction, they had taken up human form and had lived here for thousands of years. She, somehow, had managed to produce a child with a human. Those of us who carried that genetic heritage weren't quite human. Not *quite*.

The fact that this distant ancestress was dead, more or less, did not keep her from meddling in the affairs of her descendants. She had latched on to a corner of my brain, keeping my mind from being one hundred per cent my own. What she intended to do with my mind was unknown. For now, she seemed to merely be squatting, as if having a hook in my mind were enough. But I knew she wouldn't be content with that for long.

If I could just find what I was looking for, maybe I could find a way to negotiate with her, get her to let go. Maybe not, but it was the only plan Brooklyn and I had managed to come up with.

We entered the museum; a tiny gift shop was to the left while exhibits cluttered the main room. Pictures graced all the walls.

"Welcome," said an elderly gentleman who was seated near the gift shop. "First time here?"

"Yes," said Brooklyn. "First time in Florida, actually. Well, *actually*, this is my first visit to a beach. I've never seen the ocean before except in movies and travel shows on tv."

The man nodded and chuckled. "Sounds like you're making the trip of a lifetime. We're glad you decided on Pass-a-Grille. This is a very historic small town, as you can see." He gestured with a hand, sweeping it slowly until he had encompassed the whole room in a single gesture.

I wandered the room while Brooklyn kept the man occupied with breathless questions. When was the town founded? Who started the museum? What was the most interesting story he'd heard about a local resident?

I felt drawn toward a side room that was decorated with many small pieces of memorabilia from World War II. One corner of the room seemed darker than the rest. I walked over and glanced in the cabinet. Inside was a wedding band, a telegram from someone's mother to her son informing him of his father's death, and a purple heart.

None of it seemed particularly interesting. I stood for a moment, concentrating on the darkness, and felt that it was centered on the floor, not the cabinet and its items.

I knelt and felt around the base of the cabinet. Toward the back of the cabinet, against the wall, was something small and rough. I picked it up. It was a small piece of shell, fractured almost like a piece of glass. It was brilliant white on one side, and a gentle pink with pale purple spots on the other. I had no idea what the full shell would have looked like, but I doubt the shell had originally had the black stain that clung to one side. The stain could have been mold but the slight frisson of electricity that ran though my fingers as I touched it clued me in as to its real nature. It was some kind of bodily secretion. The blood of one of the Forlorn, who were the aliens like my boss and the Queen Bitch. Or maybe a tear.

Or, hell, maybe piss. Did it matter?

Some Forlorn had held onto this while bleeding, or crying, or whatever, and then dropped it here. Or they'd lost it on the beach and it had been carried in by a child, or inside someone's shoe. There must be a hundred explanations for how it could have gotten here.

The main question I wanted answered was, whose bodily fluid had stained it? And how much power did it contain?

My boss, Ware, had been collecting things he referred to as talismans. These were items imbued with supernatural power by being part of one of his kind. The Queen Bitch's tooth. A pink stone that had originally been a drop of Marveaux's blood. One of the feathers from Fish's wings. Ware had been collecting them in order to hold as much power as possible when hostilities broke out, as the Queen Bitch had prophesied they would.

That was before she had taken the sinkhole, a small pocket dimension, where Ware stored the things he wanted to keep for their power. Now all that power belonged to Zireya, the Queen Bitch.

Ware would be desperate to acquire more talismans. He'd want this bit of shell, and he'd want it badly. The next question was, would I give it to him?

Maybe I should go back to the shore and throw it in the ocean. Let whomever wanted it go swimming for it. Let the tides carry it wherever they would. Let it go.

I was under no obligation to give it to Ware. I didn't know how to use it myself. That seemed to leave ditching it in the ocean as the best course of action. Then no one could use it.

I pocketed the shell fragment and went back to the main room where Brooklyn was asking questions about local legends about the supernatural.

"So, are there any ghost stories about this place?" she asked. "Or around town in general?"

"Well, if you go to the Don Cesar—that's the pink hotel just north of here—you should keep an eye for the Smiling Man. He's supposed to be the ghost of the original owner. He's friendly; just keeping an eye on the place."

"That sounds interesting," said Brooklyn. "I don't hear too many stories about friendly ghosts."

"Jack Kerouac is supposed to haunt Haslam's Book Store. That's on Central Avenue," continued the gentleman. He had certainly warmed to the subject. I walked toward the gift shop and looked carefully at several bead necklaces. I wasn't tempted by them, but it only seemed polite to investigate the items that were for sale. Between Brooklyn's fascination with local legends, and me checking out the items that were for sale, we should be the docent's favorite people before we knew it.

"Jack Kerouac," said Brooklyn slowly. "He was a writer, right?"

The old man, whose nametag read DUANE, laughed. "Yeah, he was a writer. You know, the Beat Generation. He wrote *On the Road*."

"Oh," said Brooklyn.

I suspected she'd never heard of the guy before, or the Beat Generation, or the book *On the Road*. Hell, I'd only heard of the book because I heard a couple of women discussing it as they needed to read it for their neighborhood book club.

They had not been enthusiastic. Apparently, they had wanted their club to choose *Eat, Pray, Love*.

I'd never been part of a book club, and had never had an interest in reading, but I felt somewhat accomplished to have heard of *On the Road*, even though I hadn't known the name of the author, and still had no idea what it was about. Being on the road, I would guess.

"Old Kerouac throws books off of shelves," said Duane.

"But what about the scary ghosts? Surely there's a phantom hitchhiker story or two. It seems like everyone has one of those."

"Hmm. The scariest one I know of is the guy at the Vinoy who stands at the foot of your bed and stares at you when you sleep."

"That's creepy," said Brooklyn. "Definitely more my type of story."

"Sorry to disappoint you about the phantom hitchhiker thing. I've heard those tales before, but I don't know of any such story from here."

"I'm intrigued by the guy who stares at you when you sleep," said Brooklyn. "Do you suppose he watched people sleep when he was alive?"

Duane looked at Brooklyn craftily. "How do you know he was ever alive? Maybe he's some kind of demon that wants to frighten people. He's supposed to be terrifying."

"Hadn't thought of that," said Brooklyn. "A demon, huh? Back home we have some tales of small imp-like demons that follow people around and bite them. Also, there's these pale humanoids that live out in the woods. If you're close enough to hear them scream, you're too close. They'll sniff you out, run you into the ground, then rip you apart and eat you."

Duane's eyebrows raised halfway up his forehead. "Now that's scary. I wouldn't want to be torn apart and eaten!"

"I've heard their screams from a distance," I said, joining the conversation for the first time. I didn't mention I'd ripped one apart with my bare hands. It was not a memory I cared to have. I'd just as soon forget the whole incident. "Terrifying is too tame a word for it. It's a sound I can hardly describe. Like, imagine a cat screaming combined with a baby crying and a lion roaring. Except that doesn't even come close. The worst is how it makes you feel. The sounds hit your ears like fingernails on chalkboard, and then that feeling slides all the way from your ears to your head, down your spine, and finally to your feet. I swear my *toes* shivered in fear."

Duane shook his head slowly. "I'm glad I haven't heard anything like that. But no, I haven't heard that kind of story."

"I have," said a familiar voice.

I turned. Madrigal "Call Me Riga" Evers stood in front of an open door which had previously been closed.

"The imp thing or the screaming thing?" asked Brooklyn.

Riga crossed her arms over her ample bosom. "There's a Rake in Sawgrass Park, or so they say. I haven't been over there to investigate."

"Sounds promising," said Brooklyn. "I'm sure we'll go there to check it out."

"I'm going tonight, me and my group," said Riga. "You should come along."

"I don't think that's a good..." said Brooklyn.

"We'd love to join you," I said. Riga and I stared at each other, eye to eye, neither one of us blinking or dropping our gaze. "Tell us where to be and when."

5

Brooklyn and I had dinner at a place called Crabby Bill's. The entire western wall of the place was windows, so there was hardly a place in the restaurant that didn't have a good view. As it was, Brooklyn and I were at a table right next to the window. I was mesmerized by the sun, which slowly grew ever closer to the horizon. Sunset came in an exuberant splash of pinks and purples.

"You can't seriously be thinking of meeting, not just Riga, but *her group* in some park you've never been to before?" asked Brooklyn after we'd ordered dinner. She'd only asked me a couple dozen times at this point. "Heck, even if she doesn't kill you, she could mug you for your wallet, if nothing else."

"For the hundredth time, she won't."

"How do you know?"

I hesitated, then shrugged. "It's just a feeling. She wants something and she thinks I have it, or that I have access to it. She won't go to Ware, but since I came to her, she can shadow me until I give up and give her what she wants."

"You think she wants to join Isya's team?"

"Who knows?"

"What do you think's in the park?"

I gave Brooklyn a long stare. "You're asking a lot of questions you already know the answer to. I have no idea what's in the park. But I'd say, if it makes creepy calls at night, it's probably a Rake."

Brooklyn ate a small bite of her fish and looked thoughtful. "What if it's something we haven't seen yet? I mean, every time we interact with the Forlorn, there's something else Ware hasn't bothered to warn you about. Rakes, scraps, shadow people...we've seen a lot of crazy shit."

I took a bite of my own fish. It was tasty, which, to be honest, was exactly as it should have been. If you order fish at a restaurant on the beach, the food ought to be fresh. So at least one thing was bothering to maintain the normality of existence.

The sun was nearly to the horizon before we left the restaurant. Brooklyn got her phone to give us directions to Sawgrass and soon enough we were on our way.

The pink and gold of the sunset played across the palm trees and even more flowering plants though these I couldn't identify. Guess you couldn't get them in small pots at Home Depot. The area was beautiful yet alien to my midwestern soul.

Sawgrass Park was closed when we arrived but Riga had warned us we'd need to park nearby and get in around the gate. We found the path she'd told us about and got in easily. Then it was a short walk to a small pavilion that hosted some informational posters and the bathrooms. I sat down at a picnic table. Brooklyn continued walking to a bridge over some kind of slough.

"Oh, hey," she called out. "There's an alligator over here!"

"No way," I said. "You can't have alligators in the park. I mean, *alligators?*"

"It's just lying in the water."

"Maybe it's fake."

"Come on, take a look. It's real enough."

I sighed and got up. It wasn't like the picnic table bench was that comfortable. Why not go see some fake alligator.

I walked to where Brooklyn stood. She was leaning forward, her mouth slightly open and smiling absently. She looked as though she had won a prize she'd never thought she'd get.

Seeing an alligator couldn't be a prize, though.

Brooklyn pointed and l looked over the edge of the bridge, fully expecting to see some kind of blow-up toy that someone had thrown in the slough. Because people and littering just go together.

But, no. There was a real goddamn alligator in the water. The tail even moved slowly back and forth as it traveled at an extremely sedate pace through the water. It was fucking real.

"Does this mean alligators aren't dangerous?" asked Brooklyn. "I always thought you'd better stay far away from them."

I shrugged. "Maybe they don't bother people if people don't bother them? I dunno. It's not like I've ever studied alligator behavior."

"Well, you showed," said a now-familiar voice.

I turned to see Riga and four others walking up from the pavilion. The four behind her looked nervous, while Riga maintained a demeanor of stolid seriousness.

"First Rake hunt?" I asked the group.

"Not many opportunities to go after them here," said Riga. "I don't know why but the Forlorn have never favored Florida."

Brooklyn crossed her arms. "So you're prepared? I know these things are hard to kill."

"Kill?" asked one of the new people. He was tall and skinny and far too pale to be native. Maybe he slathered sun block on religiously to keep a burn, or a tan, at bay. I guess he wouldn't be worrying about skin cancer.

"What else are you going to do with one of those?" asked Brooklyn. "It'll eat you alive if you give it a chance. Don't give it the chance."

The tall skinny guy glanced at the redheaded woman next to him. "Nobody said anything about killing."

"Or being eaten alive," said the redhead. "Riga?"

Riga glared at Brooklyn. "Rakes are dangerous, sure. But we can handle a single Rake."

"Let's hope so," I said. "They're tough and strong."

The redhead glanced back toward the entrance to the park. "Maybe this was a bad idea."

"It was," I said. "If you're not armed to the teeth and ready to use every weapon available to you, leaving is a good plan."

The other two who had come with Riga had already faded back into the darkening twilight.

A wretched screech sounded out from the woods behind us. The sound made my entire spine shiver uncontrollably. A Rake. That call was something I never needed to hear again.

"That's enough for me," said the redhead.

The tall guy nodded. Then both turned and ran, leaving Riga as the lone remaining person from her "group."

"Are we staying?" asked Brooklyn. "Teryl's faced these things before, but I haven't, and I'm not inclined to rush in when there's only three of us."

I should have felt the same. Rakes were damn terrifying. Yet now that the initial wave of fear had passed, I found myself strangely eager to go find this thing.

I sized up Riga. She didn't appear to be frightened, which was strange. Anyone in their right mind should be terrified, just like her four friends who had already shown their native intelligence by leaving.

Maybe the woman had a death wish.

"Let's go find this thing," I said.

"We don't have to worry about alligators, right?" asked Brooklyn.

Riga snorted. "Alligators rarely bother people. The Rake is what we're after."

"To kill it," I said.

Riga finally wore an expression that wasn't supreme self-confidence. It looked like confusion. "Kill? I mean to trap it."

"Why?" Brooklyn sounded confused.

I was confused as well, but didn't bother to ask. Riga wasn't the stablest person I'd ever met; no doubt she had some crazy notion of taming it or something. Maybe experimenting on it? Who knew.

"Why?" Riga asked with some asperity. "Because it knows where the sinkhole is. It has to."

"Why does it have to?"

"Because Rakes used to be people. Special people, descended from the Queen of the Forlorn."

I shook my head, unable to listen to more. "That's scraps, not Rakes. Rakes are people who were given power but died before the power could be taken back."

Riga's eyes widened. Either she didn't like what I'd said, or didn't like being corrected. Oh well.

Riga looked over at Brooklyn, who shrugged. "Hey, I'm not one of Bitch Queen's descendants. Don't have powers, either. I'm just kind of along for the ride."

The scream of the Rake rose again from behind us. Riga grimaced. I knew the feeling; that shriek was enough to make anyone shiver with fear.

Except I wasn't shivering this time. It seemed the lack of emotion over the rest of my life had encompassed hearing Rake screams, too. That had to be a bad sign, but for the moment, I was just glad I didn't have an emotional reaction to that scream. I remembered what it was like, and I preferred not to feel like that ever again.

"I'll ask again," I said. "Why capture it if you can kill it?"

Riga blinked slowly. "I didn't know they could be killed. Ware never mentioned it."

"And none of his associates told you, either?"

"None of them spoke to me," said Riga. "You've mentioned some names, but those aren't familiar to me. Marveaux? Garnett? Mink? Who are they?"

"Whoa, Ware really kept you in the dark," said Brooklyn.

"He doesn't share much," I said. "I've usually gotten info out of him only when he feels he has no other choice than to spill."

"The drinking club, which has disbanded," said Brooklyn, "was Oya, Truck, Yama, and some other chick."

"Lucy," I said. "And, if anyone had introduced Oya to you, they would have called her Little Girl."

"She's the tall black Amazon chick," said Brooklyn. "Lucy was the dumpy one with the 60s fashion sense. Long stringy hair, peasant skirts, that kind of stuff."

"I remember them. Why did they stop meeting?"

"Oh, some of them want to resign with Isya," said Brooklyn. "Which, obviously, is bad. Also Oya went MIA after the Thunderer was born and kidnapped."

Riga shook her head slowly. "I don't even understand what you are talking about."

The Rake screeched again. Brooklyn's eyes got wide, "Sounds like it's closer."

"Maybe," I said. "Hard to say. We might as well go track it down and kill it, though."

"Why kill it?" asked Riga. "Why are you determined to end it? It didn't do anything wrong."

"Why do you care?" asked Brooklyn. "The thing used to be a person, and now they're trapped in this horrific existence. Killing it releases it from a hellish afterlife."

"How do you know it's so hellish?"

I snorted. "You've heard it. You think anything that knows happiness or contentment would scream like that? The thing is screeching out its agony."

Riga seemed to withdraw into herself, and said nothing. I shrugged. "I'm going to go kill it. I'll be back."

Brooklyn looked worried but she wasn't stupid. She'd let me face it alone so I didn't have to worry about her safety. She was just a regular person. I, well, I wasn't, even if I didn't know the extent to which I wasn't regular.

Riga took a step forward.

"Wait, you're *going?*" asked Brooklyn. "Wait here with me, why don't you. Teryl's killed one before."

Riga was pale with terror; even in the dimming twilight I could see that. But she shook her head. "No. I'm going to confront it. I have to."

I didn't know why she thought that, and didn't care. I just shrugged, turned around, and headed out over the wooden bridge into the park. I heard Riga's hollow-sounding steps on the bridge behind me but didn't turn around.

Shortly after crossing the bridge, I was confronted with a choice. Left or right. I had no idea which way would be better to go.

"If you go right," Riga said, "you'll end up in the drier section where the ground is solid. To the left it's more swampy. If you hop the railing, you'll end up sinking in the mud. So would the Rake, unless they can magically walk on top of soft mud."

"Fine. We search right first."

I turned and walked down the path, which remained wooden and elevated and bounded by handrails. The darkness under the trees was nearly absolute now.

Riga turned on a flashlight, which made me blink and realize how much of my night vision she had just ruined.

"Turn that off," I said.

"It's too dark to see."

I almost said, "no, it isn't," but I realized she was right. I should have been blind in the gloom, but I hadn't even noticed I had been able to see. Not like it was daytime, but I hadn't been blind.

"Why isn't it screaming?" asked Riga.

"Dunno. Maybe it found someone to eat."

"Someone?"

"They eat people, you know. Little kids mostly. Maybe because they can't fight back very well, or can't run fast. But when you read about kids going missing, it's probably Rakes. That's one way to track their movements, unfortunately."

"Three children went missing a few miles north of here last month." Riga sounded like the words were dragged out of her.

"That sounds about right."

Suddenly, the scream of the Rake reverberated through the woods. The call stabbed me right through the spine. It was so close that the sound got to me, freezing every nerve and spearing its way into the very marrow in my bones.

I spotted a ghastly white figure running right toward us through the undergrowth, which didn't seem to slow it down at all.

The Rake.

,

6

A strange feral joy enveloped me. I screamed my response to the Rake, and launched myself over the railing.

The thing didn't even hesitate. It kept barreling toward me, knocking down ferns and stomping half-rotted sticks underfoot. It opened its maw, displaying a mouth full of sharp teeth. It looked like the mouth of a piranha. I had no idea what crazy magic had turned a human mouth full of molars and incisors into something with a few dozen teeth all shaped like fangs.

The two of us slammed into each other like we were WWE fighters. The Rake's flesh was cold and slick. Our bodies careened off each other and I fell onto the wet soft ground. This might be the solid area of the park, but the soil here certainly wasn't all that firm.

I picked myself up but the Rake was quicker; it launched itself at me again and spun me around. I twisted my ankle around a tree root and stumbled backward into the boardwalk I'd just leaped off of.

I growled and grabbed the Rake by the throat before it could latch its teeth onto me. It bellowed and snapped its jaws together several times like some kind of demented puppet. I just kept my grip.

With my other hand, I punched the thing in the gut. Its soft flesh gave way before my fist. It pushed itself backward and I lost my grip on its neck.

"Find something to stab it with," I shouted to Riga. I thought she must still be around; I saw the light from her flashlight dancing around the area.

The thing launched itself at me and I grabbed at it but its slippery flesh slid between my fingers. The Rake closed its teeth around my left shoulder.

I screamed. I tried pulling away but the teeth were buried in my flesh deep enough that I could only get away by ripping most of the muscle away from my shoulder. Another scream rose in my throat but I swallowed it back down, leaned in toward the Rake, and grabbed the thing around the throat. My fingers pressed into its neck, harder and harder.

I wasn't sure a Rake really needed to breathe but it couldn't do much without a head. I squeezed the thing's neck with all my strength, rage overcoming me so thoroughly that the pain in my shoulder no longer mattered. The ground under my feet was nothing; the tree trunk behind me was unworthy of notice. Only the feel of the flesh of the Rake's neck shredding under my fingers was important.

I was going to rip it apart, no matter what it cost me. The fury inside me needed to be released; it flowed through my bones, burning me from the inside out. The sensation felt as if it moved up from the earth itself, charred the marrow inside my bones before heading for my lungs and exiting my body through my breath.

The air around me became tinged with the red of my rage and the brilliant orange and yellow of my fury. In contrast, the Rake became darker as its neck disintegrated under my fingers.

The Rake screamed, but I was far too gone in my anger to feel fear now. I hissed at the goddamn thing and bent my head forward so I could grab its ear with my teeth. I bit it hard, and pulled the ear away from the rest of the head.

At last, my fingers met. I closed my fists and pulled the flesh of the thing's neck in opposite directions. The Rake let go of my shoulder and I fell to the soggy fern-covered ground.

I panted from my exertion while the intense rage I'd felt slid away from me, leaving me cold and shivering, even in the damp heat of the evening. A deep satisfaction filled my heart. Score: me, 2. Rakes, 0.

The pasty white flesh shimmered briefly in the moonlight before dissolving into a pile of what looked like wet rags.

"What did you do?" asked Riga. "What did you *do*?"

"I killed it," I said. "You could say, I put it out of its misery."

"Its misery?"

I climbed to my feet slowly. My jeans were wet from sitting on the soggy ground, and mud had seeped into my shoes. Gross.

"Yeah," I said. "You heard it crying. It was the manifestation of a human soul that was trapped in this monstrous form because some irresponsible alien claimed to love it and gave it some power. Probably thinking it was being generous."

I climbed back onto the boardwalk. "I need a shower."

I started back down the boardwalk toward the cars. My shoulders ached and my hands were sticky with whatever the flesh of the Rake had been made of. I tried not to think about its bloodless white slimy flesh and what was on my hands.

A sharp crack sounded as I felt something strike me on the head. I stumbled and turned around. Riga had a thin branch in her hands; no doubt she'd picked it up from the scrub. It was broken in half with the two halves joined together with a few strands of bark that hadn't quite separated yet.

Riga tossed it down. "You killed it. I said I wanted to capture it, but you killed it instead."

"Yeah," I said. "Not only will it eat any kids in the area, but whatever was left of the person it had been before death was trapped in that wretched form. It was nothing but eternal hunger for human flesh. I guess if it went after sewer rats, we'd be giving it a medal. But that's not its preferred meal. How many "missing children" posters do you want to see dotting the neighborhood?"

Riga hesitated.

I took the opportunity to turn back around. "I'm going back to the car. Then I'm going to my hotel room and I'm going to sleep for a day. Maybe a week."

"Why did I even ask you to come?" wailed Riga.

I shook my head and did not stop. I was going to the car, because the car could take me to a shower and a bed. Hot water sluicing down on my head and shoulders sounded like perfection. Heaven.

I head footsteps behind me but I didn't turn around. I couldn't see what Riga could do to me except push me or hit me again with an undersized blunt object.

"Don't hit me again," I said. "I'll push you off this boardwalk and into the mud. It'll ruin your shoes. It's also colder than it has any right to be."

Riga shouted, "Why should I be worried about my shoes? Do you know what you've done?"

"Killed a Rake. Or, if you prefer, released a human soul from the eternal misery of cannibalistic hunger and despair."

"So you're a hero, are you? Saving babies from being eaten by a Rake." Her voice held all the tears her eyes had not yet shed.

"I'm not a hero," I said. "Whatever you mean by that word, anyway. I just killed a supernatural creature that would probably begged you, if it could have spoken, to release it from its terrible existence."

"You don't know anything about it," the other woman hissed. Her footsteps got nearer and more frequent; she was practically jogging in order to keep up with me.

"Apparently more than you," I said tiredly. "You got scraps and Rakes confused, and they're nothing alike."

"Scraps are harmless," she said.

"Try making one happy after it's decided you've insulted it," I said. My heart ached slightly. I'd had a scrap follow me around for a while like a little dog. I'm sorry to say I'd treated it like a dog. Maybe worse. And now it was gone.

"You have experience with them."

"You could say that. Just don't get them near Zireya. She'll eat them up just as surely as that Rake would have eaten any baby in its vicinity."

At last, I spotted the parking lot. Almost there. Almost free of this annoying woman and her weird fondness for Rakes.

My curiosity finally kicked in. "So, you wanted to capture this Rake."

"Yes."

"And do what with it? Medical experiments? Like, mad scientist stuff?"

Riga didn't say anything right away.

"OK, not medical experiments," I said. "Maybe you got some kids in your neighborhood you wanted to feed to it? Keep it in the basement or something. Very horror movie."

A quiet sigh came from the woman. "You wouldn't understand."

"Quite possibly not," I said. "But it seems difficult to have a sympathetic view of Rakes. I mean, it's not their fault they turned into that after death."

"Then whose fault is it?"

"The Forlorn who shared their power with a human and then never reclaimed it. I don't know which one it was that did this to the human, but it's their fault."

"The sharing of power?"

"No, the inability, or unwillingness, to think ahead. To realize, hey, this person's getting older, or is sick, so I'd better reclaim my power before I birth another Rake into the world."

"You sound so sure of yourself," she said.

"Whatever. I'm leaving." I crossed the small bridge separating the bulk of the park from the picnic area and parking lot. I waved at Brooklyn. She perked up and waved back.

"Now, if you'll excuse me, I've got a shower to take, and jet lag to get over."

"I'll never forgive you," said Riga. Her voice was low and cold as ice.

"Weird thing to say. Look, I'm tired and I have to go."

"You don't understand," she said again. "You killed him."

My ears perked up a little at that. A Rake with gender? Were all Rakes *him* to Riga or just this one.

"Him?"

"My husband. Ben."

I stopped just short of the car. Brooklyn had already gotten in and started the engine. Over its humming, I turned back to Riga slowly.

"Say again?"

The woman was crying. She'd dropped her stick so she simply looked ridiculous and sad.

"My husband. Ben. He got a Forlorn to grant him some of its eternal life so that he could live with cancer. But even that only worked for a short time. At first, it was a gift. The cancer went into remission. He came home from hospice and *lived*. For two years, we took every day by the horns and made it give us whatever would make us happy. We didn't waste a moment. And then he was gone."

"Sorry," I said. Honestly, what could I say besides that?

"That night, the funeral home reported his body stolen. The place was messed up. Tables flipped, refrigerators raided, windows broken. But it wasn't body snatchers. He'd morphed into this....thing."

"You should be grateful, then, that he's finally, truly dead, and no longer suffering. You wanted to bring him home? See if you could keep him with you by, what, feeding him hamburgers? It wouldn't have worked.'

"He could have stayed in the back room. He could have..."

"Riga," I said sharply. "He broke out of a morgue. He trashed the place, and I bet some of the stuff he did was far beyond the strength of any ordinary person. He was *strong*. Supernaturally strong. You couldn't have kept him on a leash like a pet."

"He should be home with me!"

"Look," I said. "Apparently, he shouldn't. I mean, yeah, that's the life you would have chosen. I suppose what he would have chosen, too. But he had cancer. He would have died of that in any case."

"People survive cancer all the time."

"Yeah, but you had him in hospice. I doubt you did that because the doctor had given you hope for his recovery."

That made her pause. I took the opportunity to get into the car. "Home, Jeeves," I said tiredly.

"Hotel it is," she said, looking critically at my clothing. "You took a bath in the mud?"

"Something like that. I'll tell you after a shower."

"Okay." She started backing out of the space.

My curiosity got the better of me again. I rolled down the window and called out to Riga. "Which Forlorn did it? Which gave up some power for Ben?"

It was too dark to see much of her face, but Riga appeared to be crying again. Still. Whatever. She glanced at me before getting in her own car. As she pulled out, she whispered just loudly enough to be heard over the car engines.

"Mink." Then she finished backing out of the space and drove away.

"Mink what?" asked Brooklyn. She'd met Mink in London.

"Mink is the one that turned her husband into that Rake."

"Oh," said Brooklyn softly. "What a bitch."

"Yeah," I said. "I'll curse her for Ben's sake, but right now, I really need that shower."

"On the way."

Brooklyn got out of the parking space, pulled out of the park, and tuned left at the main street.

The few miles to the hotel were far longer than they had any right to be. I admitted it, I felt badly for Riga. She was an unpleasant person now, but I could see her being loyal to her husband, overjoyed when he had a second chance, and devastated when it all came crashing down. Hell, I'd probably be a bitch who hit people over the head with bats, too.

Once in the shower, I leaned against the wall and let the falling hot water substitute for the tears I couldn't shed.

7

"So, what do we do next?" asked Brooklyn after I'd cleaned up and we'd gotten some dinner from the Burger King next door to the hotel.

"Back to the museum, I suppose," I said. "There's that black cloud hanging over it and we need to know how it marks the sinkhole. If it marks the sinkhole."

"And if it does, then what? We just nod to ourselves and go home? We try to destroy it? We open it up and have tea with whomever's inside?"

I shook my head. How was I supposed to know?

"We'll go back in the morning," I said. "Who knows, maybe we can figure something out. I don't know if I can sense anything more, but we won't know if we don't try."

"Okay," said Brooklyn. "I'm exhausted, anyway. A few hours' sleep will be fantastic. Why is airline travel so hard on you?"

I decided that question was rhetorical and laid down on one of the queen beds in the hotel room without answering. The room was frigid and I thought briefly of playing with the controls, but Brooklyn had already done that a couple of times to no effect. Didn't matter, anyway. My life was a mess; being uncomfortably hot or cold had to be the least of my worries.

My mind ranged back to London, where Brooklyn and I had spent some time with Mink. I'd thought she was going to help us, but it turned out she was on the other side. I couldn't keep everyone's motivations and loyalties straight and resented that I probably should pay more attention. It was just that, the last time these immortal beings had gone to war, they'd managed to destroy entire galaxies. What chance did *Earth* have if they decided to take up where they left off?

Let's face it, if they decided to take up violence again, humanity was screwed. No ifs, ands, or buts.

Mink had a sweet, docile appearance in her human form, which clearly did not reflect the creature underneath. That creature had arcane powers that a human like me could hardly counter. Or understand.

I slept fitfully and finally got up around three a.m. Brooklyn was quietly snoring so I snuck out of the room as quietly as possible and walked to the lobby. The front desk was dark though I saw a light coming from underneath an office door. I suppose if anyone showed up, they could get checked in by whomever was staffing the office during the night shift.

The TV in the breakfast area was showing some old movie that looked like it was from the sixties, judging by the crazy hairstyles and lack of bras on any of the actresses. I tried watching it for a few minutes but the storyline was difficult to determine without sound and the visuals were uninteresting.

I sighed and decided to go for a walk. The area around the hotel seemed well-kept and even at this time of night, traffic was fairly dense. Like many cities these days, the sheer quantity of light outside made the darkness look more gloomy than anything. Only a few stars could be viewed through the light pollution of St. Petersburg.

I checked to make sure I had my phone in my pocket, as well as my room key card. Satisfied I was as prepared as I could be for an impromptu walk around the block, I left the lobby and stepped into the humid air. The thick atmosphere was full of sweet scents, no doubt from all the flowery plants around the hotel's parking lot, and the faint smell of salt. The smell was unusual to my Midwestern nose, but not unpleasant.

I walked around the parking lot for a few minutes, wondering how crazy I'd look to someone watching. But an insomniac taking a walk around a hotel parking lot had to, actually, be one of the least idiotic things I could be observed doing, I supposed.

I glanced back at the hotel entrance but I didn't want to re-enter the building. I needed to get away. That didn't make sense; I had come here with Brooklyn because I needed her to ground me and guide me while my mind was fragile and unbalanced. Zireya's hold on me was tight, though at least I could still fight it. Not well, but I could.

Thoughts of Zireya made me think of deep space and the cold that the Forlorn had traveled in for eons. The cold and dark of space. For a human, it was terrifying: too large to comprehend, too empty to be comfortable, too alien to be home.

And yet my heart ached with my desire to regain a freedom I personally had never had. I shook my head and glanced around, noticing for the first time that the hotel had vanished.

Or, more accurately, it was somewhere behind me. I had daydreamed of space and a life lived in the void between the stars, and had wandered away from anything familiar. I glanced at a nearby street sign, but that didn't help. It seemed this city had all the main streets numbered, with thoroughfares marked *street* and those marked *avenue* running north-south and east-west, respectively. Or maybe it was the other way around.

In any case, I had no idea what street the hotel was on, so the fact I had just passed a road called 58th Street did not help me in any way.

A car pulled in a parking lot just in front of me. I wouldn't have noticed it except for the odd flute music coming from its open windows. The effect of the haunting Indian-inspired music juxtaposed with the salt air and palm trees of Florida was absurd.

Of course, that begged the question of what kind of music a random car *should* have coming from its interior while tooling around Florida.

Jimmy Buffett, I guess. Or maybe steel drums.

A tall man got out of the car. A man I recognized.

Oh shit.

Aditya.

Aditya and I had fought when I'd gone to London to find an item Ware wanted returned to his possession. I'd known I couldn't kill him, or even do him serious damage, but somehow, I hadn't expected to see him again.

Much less to see him in Florida. Dressed in an orange-and-pink Hawaiian shirt with bright yellow pineapples all over it.

I guess the garish shirt meant blending in when in Florida, but anywhere else, and it was a nightmare of colors and patterns.

Well, and Hawaii. Florida and Hawaii. Otherwise, such shirts were definitely a fashion don't.

Feeling particularly bold, or ridiculously idiotic, I sauntered up to the car. Aditya stood next to it, waiting patiently for me to come to him. That annoyed me. What was he doing here, and why couldn't he just leave me alone?

"Aditya," I said as I grew close.

"Teryl," he replied with a slight nod. His hair, which before had been plaited down his back, was piled on top of his head with a few bits of shiny metal sticking out. It looked as if his head were a pincushion. The effect was weirdly exotic but also funny, as if he'd hurriedly twisted his hair around his head and stuck bits of metal into his scalp.

"I thought hatpins went through hats, not your head," I said.

He patted his hairstyle gingerly. "I didn't feel like doing anything elaborate. I'd heard you were coming to St. Petersburg, and I gather I know what for, but following you in a timely manner was a bit difficult."

"Hard to pack light when you've got so many colors to get in the luggage," I said.

He looked down at his shirt critically. "I like this one. But no, what I meant was, Ware was worried about you and so I volunteered to come keep an eye on you. But then, Brooklyn bought the tickets and it took me a bit of detective work to figure out where the two of you were headed, and when."

"Last time we spoke," I said slowly, "you were opposing Ware."

He shrugged. "Not really. I just oppose the idea of restarting ancient conflicts, especially when such a beautiful planet would end up being destroyed in the process."

"That's nice. So why did you decide to pull over now?"

"Because I'm tired of following you in a car while you're walking. If you're going somewhere in particular, let me know and I'll meet you there. Or I'll give you a lift, assuming you'd even get in the car."

"You could just follow me on foot."

Aditya's chiseled features pulled back in an expression of disgust. "Walk? Why should I do that?"

"Oh, I dunno. You were just complaining about having to drive too slowly to suit you. So walk instead."

He just shook his head. "Ware should just hire an entire cadre of bodyguards to follow you around. Why he thinks I should do it is a mystery."

"Indeed," I said. "I don't know that I believe you and he are even on speaking terms, let alone that you'd be doing him favors."

"Maybe I was bored."

"Maybe I don't believe you."

He shrugged. "Fine. So, are you going anywhere? I could take you."

"And listen to that horrendous music?"

He sighed dramatically. "I can turn the music off. Come on, where are you headed?

I didn't want to admit I had no idea. "Where do you think?"

"Oh, probably back to that museum. You seemed quite interested in it. Did you notice something odd there?"

I couldn't tell if he was trying to draw me out or just confirm something he already knew, so I shrugged. "What's it to you?"

"I'd say nothing, but that's hardly believable. Look, I get that you're angry at Ware. I even get that you'd want to get ahead of him on this. That's exactly what Zireya would have done: Ware always followed her. He was never the leader. Now that she and you have some kind of....arrangement...I suppose you becoming more active in seeking out Isya was inevitable."

I knew I shouldn't even contemplate getting in his car, but my new lack of regard for my safety was too strong to resist. "Sure. Yeah, why not. Let's go to the museum."

Aditya nodded and opened the car door for me. I slid into the passenger seat and let him pilot me toward the beach.

The strange cloud that hung over the museum seemed to rise in my mind, like a kind of beacon. Eyes open or eyes shut, I felt its presence ahead. The knowledge of where it was in relation to myself was like putting a pin in a map. There was a pin in the museum, and another in my head, and they were tied together somehow.

I didn't like thinking about it. But I sat back and let Aditya do the driving, while the night drew around us like a shroud.

8

The call of the dark cloud above the museum got louder the closer we got. Behind the strange siren call was a more rhythmic sound like the crashing of the waves on the beach.

"Parking will be a breeze," said Aditya. "Maybe I should be happy you decided to wander about in the middle of the night rather than wait until rush hour."

I didn't answer that. Instead, I paid more attention to the passing buildings and neighborhoods than I had when Brooklyn had driven us to the beach. Much of the area seemed filled to the brim with strip malls featuring cell phone carriers, Chinese restaurants, and small convenience stores. If I were in the market for cheap cigarettes, liquor, lottery tickets, or cold water, I had it made. I could have bought those items from at least one store on every block.

"Back in the old days," I said, "what did you think of Ware and Isya? What was Zireya like? Why did you let her convince you to come to Earth, give up your wings, and appear human?"

A sharp bark of laughter escaped my companion. "Those are not easy questions to answer. Ware and Isya? They were completely different from each other both in personality and appearance, yet they also seemed a similar as twins."

"That's unnecessarily contradictory."

Aditya shook his head. "No. If you'd ever seen them together, you'd know what I meant. Ware was always stocky and solid, like something immovable. His feathers were the most brilliant white, yet each was tipped in the deepest black. Isya was slim and wiry, with black wings. Every feather had a small white edge to it just at the very end. His wings looked like the night sky: a black background covered in tiny shining points. So superficially, they looked almost opposite."

When he stopped speaking for a few moments to pull the car into a left turn lane and turn on the turn signal, I prompted him to continue. "Okay, and then what?"

"Well, they might have looked different but each gave off this aura of raw power you could *feel* right in your gut from a great distance away. When either turned his attention to you, you couldn't do much besides stand there, almost like you were transfixed by the sheer force of their personality. None of the rest of us had personalities like that. Some, like the Tunneler, hardly seemed to have power or personality at all. Others, like Mink or Little Girl, came across as strong, but not so much that you were shocked into paralysis whenever you got near them."

Interesting. I'd found Little Girl, who had told me to call her Oya, quite intimidating. She was tall and forceful and clearly did not suffer fools. Mink had seemed quite ordinary. I couldn't remember being affected by her personality any more than I was by an average person on the street.

Aditya continued. "In the beginning, Isya had a larger following than Ware. He advocated a more hands-on approach to the universe: he wanted us to rule it. He wanted to seek out life, encourage the development of intelligence, and direct that life. He wanted to be a god."

Great. An immortal powerful creature who liked playing god. Sounded like Isya had been a treat to know back in the day. "And Ware?"

"At first, he seemed to want the same, but eventually, it turned out he didn't have that much interest. He paid attention if Isya found other life, especially if it had some rudimentary intelligence, but he didn't seek it out himself."

"And he wanted to be a god, too?"

"Yes. Well, somewhat. But over time, he lost interest in that, too. While Isya wanted to lord our divine natures over every other species, Ware couldn't be bothered. He'd observe and he'd tell us we should appreciate others for the way they developed all on their own. That we shouldn't bother them, or try to direct them. Most certainly, he didn't support the idea of having them worship us."

That was a bit of a relief, assuming Aditya was telling me the truth. I had at times feared Ware, or been awed by him, but I had respected him. Well, sometimes, anyway. It would be difficult for me to respect him in the future if I were always thinking he secretly wanted to be worshiped.

The salt smell became stronger and I saw water ahead. "Almost there?"

"A few more miles," he said. "Pass-a-Grille is at the southernmost tip of the peninsula. We'll be turning left again soon and then go straight until the land ends."

"Since when are you so familiar with St. Petersburg?"

"I've been lots of places," he said. "When you're immortal, you end up going many places on multiple occasions. Personally, I prefer the Indian Ocean. But the Gulf is nice. It's generally very calm, not all gray and angry like the Atlantic."

"Huh. I've never been to the beach, let alone tried to compare them."

"Perhaps you'll get to do more traveling in the future."

I didn't say that it didn't seem like I was going to have a future, considering how his kind kept mucking about in my life. If I, or anyone else on this planet, was going to have a future, we had to keep Ware and Isya from going to war again.

I hoped that was what Zireya wanted, too. If she were going to muck about in my *mind*, then her motives better be worth the invasion of privacy. I could forgive a lot if I could just sure she wanted to save the world. Save humans.

Save me.

It's great that some people, and many fictional characters, are willing to sacrifice themselves for others, but I wasn't that selfless or brave. I wanted to live.

9

I stood in the street, staring at the museum building. I had no idea what I was looking for.

Aditya stood to the side. His posture wasn't submissive, exactly, but his body language was much different from what I remembered in London. There, he had been arrogant, confident. Here, he seemed a little lost. Maybe even nervous.

"You didn't get along with the Queen Bitch or something?" I asked.

Aditya raised his gaze to meet mine. His face went from unsure to anxious. I could swear he was sweating, and the temperature was quite temperate.

"You were afraid of her."

He blinked and a touch of the anxious slid off his face. He shrugged. "Everyone was. Well, maybe not Ware and Isya. Or maybe they just hid it better. But she was...terrifying. Beautiful, gifted, intelligent, creative, generous. She was so many things. But under it all, she had a strength none of us could match. And I don't just mean she was physically stronger."

That didn't surprise me. Zireya had to have had an absolute fucking iron fortress for a heart. A solid iron core to her soul that was indestructible. That didn't seem right; iron was probably not strong enough a metaphor. Maybe titanium?

"What's the strongest metal?" I asked idly. The stars twinkled overhead and the distant sound of the waves crashing on shore just a few yards away made the question sound ridiculous. I was standing in the middle of the street contemplating a supernatural hole in the universe while nature surrounded me, and I was asking random questions about items on the periodic table?

If that didn't show how messed up I was getting, what would?

"Depends," said Aditya. "Tungsten has the highest tensile strength. For sheer hardness, chromium. For strength plus low density, titanium."

Well. I *had* asked.

"And you know this because?"

He snorted. "You get that I was birthed eons ago, right? I've watched stars go nova and spill the molecules that make up your body into the universe. The elements that make up everything, except hydrogen, is created in the hearts of stars. Well, and helium. The rest are made when stars die."

"That doesn't necessarily mean you know everything about chemistry, or physics, or whatever. If I'd asked Ware, would he have known the answer?"

Aditya laughed this time, though his face remained unsure. He reminded me of a mouse not knowing what way to run when the cat was nearby.

"I don't know what Ware does and doesn't know," he said. "But I know because the elements that make up you, me, this street, that beach, the ocean...they are *poetry*. They are music. They are the notes the universe plays to create the song we call existence. Did you know that the iron in your blood killed a star?"

"Don't be ridiculous," I said, and turned my attention back to the museum. I was glad this town was so small; no cars had come by. No joggers had come down the street. Despite being surrounded by hundreds of thousands of people, it was as if Aditya and I were alone in our own tiny universe. Alone and having the weirdest conversation.

"It's true," he said. "In the last moments of a star's life, it begins to, well, I anthropomorphize, but it begins to panic. In its death spasms, helium is changed to lithium, then beryllium, boron, carbon, nitrogen, oxygen, and so on until the star gets to iron. The millisecond that happens, the star explodes. Lack of fuel causes a star to die, but iron is the substance that does the deed. Your blood runs through your veins with the remains of that star's death throes."

His voice had become slightly lower, his words almost sing-song in their delivery. Nothing in the one chemistry class I'd taken in high school could have prepared me for the way my heart sang to his words. How my breath got caught up in the flow of the sounds of their names. How deeply poignant the thought of my star-killer blood was. How amazing everything he had said was.

He was right. Elements were a kind of poetry. The universe, a place of chemistry and physics, was, at its core, a form of poetry. Not just cold. Not just dark. Not just empty. But beautiful and awesome and so wondrous the mere thought of it took my breath away.

I blinked and the feeling faded. Sure, the universe was poetry, but only when a supernatural creature was making some kind of pretty spell out of his words. I could see why this particular Forlorn loved music. He could use the music of his words to affect others strongly.

"Great," I said. "Human blood exists because stars died. Someone needs to make a shirt that reads *A star died and all I got was this lousy t-shirt.*"

He was silent for a few moments. A light breeze teased its way through my hair. I enjoyed the salt scent on the air and the caress of the breeze. The beach was turning out to be a pretty nice place. Too bad I wasn't here for pleasure. Maybe, if I lived through whatever madness was headed my way, I could come back. I could use something to look forward to, because since I first got involved with the Forlorn, I had been tied up in knots knowing something was coming for me that was more dangerous that I could imagine. Surviving did not seem too likely.

"Well," he said at last. "Well. I have to say that's not the reaction most humans have after listening to me."

"Is it cliché for me to say I'm not most humans?"

"Yes," he said. "But it's also true."

I sighed. I wasn't accomplishing anything by just staring at the building. "There's no one around. I'm going to check around the place. See if I can sense anything."

Aditya said nothing, and I didn't need his permission, anyway, so I left him behind and walked toward the building. The yard was just gravel; a few palm trees and spiky bushes were the only things breaking through that layer of rock. My footsteps on the gravel made a noise louder than anything else in this peaceful night. I wasn't going to be sneaking up on anything.

I heard Aditya say something softly; despite the low volume he sounded annoyed, maybe even angry. I turned around.

Two Forlorn stood on the street watching me. Aditya, of course. But the other one was also known to me: Mink.

10

I stalked back to the Forlorn, putting aside my plan to explore the area around the museum building.

"What the fuck are you doing here?" I asked as I approached the creatures.

Mink giggled, which made a flash of anger stab me in the heart. I felt like I were choking on indignation that could quickly turn into rage if I weren't careful.

"I'll take that smile off your face," I said. My voice was almost a growl.

To my surprise, Mink's face actually fell. I couldn't believe one gruff statement from a lowly human could affect her, but Aditya took a step back. Both of them had reacted poorly. Something was up.

"What's wrong?" I asked Aditya. As I swung my gaze toward him, he took another step back. His face was back to showing anxiety. Maybe even outright terror.

"Wrong?" he asked in a voice thin and reedy, unlike his usual speaking voice.

"Yeah, what's fucking wrong?" When Aditya said nothing, I turned on Mink. She looked almost as scared.

"Zireya?" she asked in a whisper. "Is that you?"

"Hardly," I said.

Mink tried a smile, but the effort only made her face contort into a grotesque caricature of a happy countenance. She gave up quickly. "I see her in your movements. I hear her in your voice. She is here." Her voice was scarcely above a whisper, as if her throat were closing in terror.

"Whatever. Why are *you* here? Is this where Ware stuck Isya? Is there a sinkhole in that black cloud that hangs over this place?"

Mink transferred her weight from foot to foot, as if she couldn't decide if answering the question were preferable to running away. Her eyes teared up. That annoyed me. Who was she to act all delicate and hurt when she was a powerful supernatural creature who could crush me with her pinky, and I was a nobody. A nobody carrying around a parasite that probably wasn't going to let me go as long as I lived. But I couldn't dwell on that right now.

"Don't run," I snarled.

Mink blinked and her eyes widened in fear. Yes, definitely fear. She feared me. Or, more correctly, she feared the shadow currently clutching at my mind.

"I...I think so," she said. "The sinkhole is the most complex one Ware ever made. It moves itself every so often so no one ever truly knows where it is. Not even Ware. He didn't trust himself to leave it alone if he could get to it."

"Leave it alone? He's got his arch-enemy in there, right? Why would he mess with that? Risk Isya escaping?"

Mink dropped her gaze to her feet. "Because the two of them were so close. Closer than brothers. He missed Isya desperately. If he had access to the sinkhole, he'd want to go inside. To meet Isya. Speak to him, even fight with him. Anything, just so they'd be together again for a little while. Even if Isya were angry, even if he were enraged at Ware, Ware would still want to be with him."

I didn't like that answer, but it rang true. Everything I knew about Ware and everything I'd heard from others about him, made what Mink said totally plausible. I remembered some line in a move about how superheroes and their arch-nemeses had generally started as friends. How their conflict grieved them both.

That was Ware and Isya. The cliches just kept rolling in.

"This sinkhole has only been here a few weeks," said Mink. She pushed hair behind her ear with a delicate hand. "I don't know how long it will be here before it moves again, so I've got to find a way in soon."

"There's only one moving sinkhole?" I asked.

Mink hesitated, then shrugged. "I can't answer that. I only know of one. I don't know one is all Ware made."

"Can't you make sinkholes, too? Maybe it's yours."

She shook her head. "I can make sinkholes but not nearly as good as Ware can. Mine are shallow. Go in one and you'd feel like you trapped in a small cage. Ware's can hold entire worlds inside. I certainly can't make one that's not anchored to the spot where I made it. If I were to make one here, it would remain here. Even if climate change raises sea level to the point where this spit of land is underwater, the sinkhole would still be here. It might fade over the ages, but it would never move."

"So if there's a sinkhole here, what do we do with it? Can you open it? Since it's Ware's, I mean."

"No," said Mink. "Even Ware can't open one of mine, and I certainly can't open one of his."

"Well, then, what's your plan? Get him to come down here before it goes away? Why would he do that?"

Mink smiled. "I don't have to. He would never open this sinkhole on purpose, anyway. But I don't need him. You're here."

11

"Say what now?" That had to be the last thing I would have expected Mink to say. "I'm just some stupid human."

"I'll agree with the stupid part," said Mink.

I shook my head. "If *you* can't open it, and you're so powerful, then I'm not going to be able to."

"Well, yes," said Mink.

I noticed Aditya looking very uncomfortable in the faint pre-dawn light. He looked as if he'd sucked on a lemon.

"What?" I asked him.

He looked at me helplessly. "Even one of the Lost couldn't open it, that's true. But you're hardly an ordinary one of the Lost, are you?"

Mink actually looked slightly giddy. "I hate her guts," she said. "I hate how she convinced us to come here, to give up our home in space. I hate how much I miss my wings. But here's one good thing: no sinkhole is proof against Zireya."

"Queen Bitch?" I said louder than I intended. Shock can do that. And surprise. But then, why was I surprised. Zireya could do pretty much anything, it seemed. Even cheat death.

"Ware couldn't stand against her," said Aditya slowly. "No sinkhole of his could stand against her, either."

"Well, then, I guess we're safe from your boss," I said to Mink. "I won't be opening any sinkholes. Not this one, not any other. Even if *she* could, even if she *would*, I wouldn't."

"You speak as if you have a choice," said Mink. "But I doubt that Zireya will let you exercise your will in any matter where your opinion or desire differs from hers."

"She can kick rocks," I said.

I walked toward the beach without a backward glance. I was not going to stand here having this ridiculous conversation. I could call Brooklyn later, see if she'd come pick me up. In the meantime, I could stand on the beach, let the salt air fill my lungs, and listen to the waves.

The strange feeling in my head, the one that had started when I'd confronted Zireya in Ware's sinkhole, ratcheted up a notch. I had almost learned to ignore it, but it seemed it was not going to ignore me.

The waves coming onto shore were shockingly small, and the noise they made was calming. It seemed to me that when I'd seen movies with the ocean in them, the waves were much higher, more powerful. The blue-green water here seemed more like a bathtub than an ocean. Maybe not every large body of water looked like it was going to kill you the moment you put your foot in it.

Plenty of things wanted me dead. The ocean needed to take a number and get in line.

I walked up the beach, letting my brain relax as the day grew brighter. The temperature started to hike up, but I didn't care. The sea breeze made it easy to ignore the rising temperature, at least for now while it was still early morning.

Shells littered the beach. I had no idea what kind they were but they were pretty. I stopped to pick up one with an interesting shape and realized while I looked at it that it was broken. But now I could see all the whorls and ledges inside the shell, and the pearly white interior contrasted beautifully with the multi-colored exterior.

I pocketed the shell and kept my eyes toward the sand, spotting one beautiful shell after another. Hundreds, thousands. Maybe millions of them lay scattered over the sand. I stopped and looked out at water. Somewhere under there, millions of small animals lived their lives and then, when they died, they decayed away and what was left of them was spit out by the ocean, piled on the beach.

While I stood staring out at the water, something caught my attention back toward where I'd come. I glanced over and saw Aditya walking the beach. I glanced around but didn't see Mink at the moment.

A few humans began walking onto the beach from the road as the sun began peeking through the low clouds in the eastern sky. As far as the locals and the tourists were concerned, today was just another beautiful day in paradise.

But the tall Indian man in a neat suit and leather shoes belied that. The supernatural was here, too, and that made the beach anything but paradise.

I turned my back to the ocean and walked awkwardly over the loose sand that separated the packed sand at the ocean's edge from the wooden stairs that led up and over the dunes. On the other side was the road. I bet there was someplace nearby that served breakfast. I'd go there and call Brooklyn, tell her where I was.

Get myself a ride away from this place.

I got to the street and did not look around to see if Aditya had followed. I was sure he planned to.

Someone waved at me from across the street. Riga.

That bitch was following me still? Fucking hell. I couldn't get away from anyone, could I?

"Come on," she called. "Breakfast is on me."

I hesitated, but why not? The woman wasn't dangerous, just annoying. Not to mention pathetic.

I hopped in her car.

Riga piloted the car out of the tiny town with the museum and toward a wide boulevard with hotels and restaurants along each side. After only a couple of miles, she pulled into a small parking area and nodded to a place called The Frog Pond. "Good breakfasts here."

"Okay." Honestly, I wasn't sure why she was driving me to get a meal, but whatever.

The sign on the door read CLOSED but even as we drew near the place, someone inside flipped it to say OPEN. We'd be the first customers, it seemed.

We sat down at a table. I ignored the menu and looked straight at Riga. "Spit it out."

"I beg your pardon?"

"Spit it out. You're being nicey-nice, which is odd for a stalker. You were pissed beyond everything after I destroyed a Rake you say was your husband. So what's up now?"

The server came over but Riga waved her away. "Please give us a few minutes."

The sever shrugged and wandered off. Since she had no other customers, I suppose she might actually have wanted to take an order. Just to have something to do, right?

I turned my attention back to Riga. "Yesterday you were practically at my throat. This morning, we're sitting down to breakfast. And the difference is...?"

Riga shifted uncomfortably in her seat. "I watched you last night. And this morning. With Mink."

"All right. And?"

"I know she wants Isya released. I believe this would be extraordinarily bad. I wanted to know how chummy you'd get with her."

"Sure."

Riga sighed. "You didn't look chummy at all. That's good. Maybe I can trust you to leave the sinkhole alone."

"I don't want Isya wandering about," I said. "You should never have thought that was a thing with me."

"But you came here to find it," she said sharply. "You traveled from St. Louis to St. Petersburg just to find it. That indicated to me that you wanted to open it."

I sat back in my chair. "Or just that I'm tired of Ware seeming to be a step, or five, ahead of me. Now that Queen Bitch has a hold on my brain, I need to know more. But I'm not sure coming here was a good idea. Mink said this sinkhole moves. So the fact it's here now doesn't mean it's going to be here next week or next month. Hell, it might take off before we're finished with breakfast."

"It won't."

She sounded so sure. "You know more about the sinkhole than Mink?"

Riga shrugged. "I listened to Ware as much as I could, eavesdropped whenever possible. He probably knew what I was up to, but he never mentioned it. So I kept at it. According to what I heard, this sinkhole does move. But only once in a while, and once Zireya puts herself back on the playing field, it won't move again until it's opened."

Zireya trying to take over my mind was "back on the playing field?" Interesting way to phrase it.

"That's nice," I said. "So what?"

The server wandered back over. This time, I just handed her the menu and said, "French toast, orange juice."

Riga handed her menu back as well. "The same."

The server looked relieved. Well, now she had something to do, I guess. Not much, but something. I saw some folks crossing the street outside and headed for the door. The server would have more to do from now on. Maybe that would suit her.

"Back to our discussion," I said. "I had just asked, *so what?*"

Riga placed both hands on the table in front of her. "Now that we know where it is, and that it will stay, any ally of Isya's will come here to try to open it. Word will eventually get back to Ware, assuming you don't tell him yourself right now."

"Yeah, sure," I said. "But that still doesn't answer the *so what* question."

"Keep an eye on that couple in the corner," said Riga. "The guy in the Beach Life t-shirt and the gal in the green tank top."

"Sure," I said. "But don't change the subject."

"I'm not," she hissed. "I've seen them before. They're not Forlorn, and may not even be Lost, but they've run errands for allies of Isya before. They may be helping Mink keep track of your location."

"So they're just like you."

"I tell you, I don't want the thing opened. They probably have no idea what happens or why they've been paid to follow you around. Doesn't matter. All we need to know is they've been paid to spy on you. They probably have no idea about the sinkhole, or who Mink is really, or what happens if Isya gets loose."

"So, they're me a couple of years ago. Before I learned anything," I mused.

"Except Ware has at least explained some things to you. These people are ignorant. They trail you, and report. That's all they're being paid for."

Our server placed our orange juices in front of us and left without speaking. Just as well; small talk wasn't my kind of thing, and today was shaping up to be way too frustrating for any kind of small talk.

"Okay, but we're going round and round here. I ask again, so what?"

"Now that the sinkhole's location is known, more people will be following you. Aditya and Mink are still watching. Ware probably has other means of figuring out your location."

"Everybody's going to so much trouble for little old me," I said with a shrug.

"The more that follow you, the more you'll find people in your path. Even your allies may hinder you if they're ignorant of the true situation."

"Okay, but...." It seemed half my sentences were starting with those two words these days.

"Some may want to keep you away. Others are going to want your help opening it. You've made more friends and enemies in the last twenty-four hours than you know."

"I wouldn't say no to a few more friends," I said.

My phone rang. I glanced at it. Brooklyn. Shit. I should have called her to update her on my location. On what was happening.

I picked up the line. "Hello? Brooklyn, hey, sorry. I'm out at breakfast..."

Mink's voice came across the line. "I'm sure you're having a great breakfast. But Brooklyn may not be having any. At least, *I* have no plans to make her life easier. It would have been better if she'd just stayed home."

"What do you think you're doing?"

"What my master always planned. I'm going to open that sinkhole. With your help. Or your friend dies the most horrible death I can work out."

12

I sat, stunned. Brooklyn was a hostage now. Mink, or some compatriot of hers, had taken her. I felt faint and my appetite disappeared. I couldn't let Mink hear my anxiety, though. Never let them see you sweat, right?

"She likes her eggs over easy," I said. "Or she'll eat cold pizza straight outta the fridge. That's what I know about her breakfast habits."

Riga frowned as the significance of this statement came across. That, and probably the lack of color in my face. I could *feel* the blood draining from my cheeks.

"Not information I need to know. I will see you tonight at the museum. We will open the sinkhole and rescue my master from his unwarranted incarceration."

Unwarranted? I could hardly agree with that. "He should stay there. We don't need you guys roaming around destroying everything in your path again. You did it once, and only one of you has paid for that. Let him continue to pay. I can't even imagine how many trillions of lifeforms you guys made extinct. How many intelligent lifeforms were on the verge of discovering farming, or flight, or space travel, never got to invent such things because one day, they were just gone. You'd make humans next."

"Dramatic," said Mink. "I'll give you that. But it's not like you're important. Not to our kind, anyway. We should reclaim our rightful place in the universe. Whether or not your kind survive is not even a footnote in that story."

"And yet here you are, unable to achieve your aims without the help of us grubby humans."

"I only need your help because of what Zireya did. She divested herself of some of her power when she bore a hybrid child. It really Zireya's legacy that I need, not your humanity. Without her donation to your genetic inheritance, you'd be like the rest of your kind: dull and witless, doomed to self-destruction."

"Thanks," I said. "Cheery. What if I say no?"

Mink sighed. "You've seen movies, right? I tell you I have your friend and that you need to do what I say or she dies. So, you do what I say."

"Sure, I've seen movies. I know that doing what you want may mean Brooklyn survives. Or you could kill her anyway. Or, hell, she might already be dead."

"You want proof of life," Mink stated baldly. "You realize you're just pissing me off for no reason. I can arrange something but I'm not inclined to."

I thought about it. Was there a point? "I bet you could mimic her voice, anyway. Or one of your friends could. Hearing her speak wouldn't be proof of anything, would it?"

I didn't know if Mink had the power to imitate humans, but the silence that followed my question answered it for me.

"I'll take that as a yes. So, I have no reason to believe she's alive, even if I hear her voice," I said. "Consequently, I will not be meeting you at the museum tonight."

My heart pounded as if it wished to leap out of my throat and rescue Brooklyn all by itself. I didn't want to see Brooklyn hurt, not on my account, but if the sinkhole opened, we'd probably all be dead, anyway. Also, there was very little Mink could do to make me think she was keeping Brooklyn alive.

Still. Throwing a friend under the bus like this wasn't something that helped one to look at oneself in the mirror every morning. I'd be looking at myself thinking *maybe you could have saved her* for the rest of my life.

"I advise you reconsider," she said at last. "I'll meet you there at one. That should provide us with enough privacy. The bar patrons at the local watering holes should have headed home by then."

I hesitated. I'd just said I wouldn't be there. I doubted I should go back on that just yet. "We'll see. If I decide to come, then I'll see you there at one. If not, then not."

Mink hung up without another word. I put my phone down. "Mink has Brooklyn," I said. "She wants to meet up tonight. She'll let Brooklyn go if I open the sinkhole."

Our server came back over with our French toast. She placed the plates down in front of us, and said sunnily, "Can I get you anything else?"

"No thanks," I said, waiting, almost breathless, for her to retreat to the kitchen. Once she was gone, Riga leaned forward and caught my eye.

"You can't open the sinkhole, not even for your friend. If Isya gets out, everyone's dead."

"That's what everyone says," I muttered as I cut the French toast into bite-sized pieces before pouring maple syrup over my plate. My stomach did a low queasy roll but I hadn't had anything to eat for hours and I was going to need some energy to face this day without sleep. I certainly couldn't do it without food as well.

"Everyone is right," said Riga. "Get on a plane and just go back to St. Louis. That should keep the damn thing closed unless Ware comes here himself."

Ware. It seems like I should update him on what was happening here. "Damn."

"What?" asked Riga.

"Ware. I should call him. He might have some advice on how to deal with Mink, or even would know who she might have on her side."

Riga's face was a mix of curiosity and disgust.

"I gather you didn't part on great terms," I said.

She shrugged and shoved French toast into her mouth. "Maybe not. But you're right. If anyone can give us advice on dealing with Mink, it would be Ware."

"Us?" I asked.

She glanced up somewhat guiltily. "Neither of us wants the sinkhole open, right? And now Mink has your friend. You could use backup."

"And, as you reminded me multiple times last night, I killed what remained of the love of your life."

Riga closed her eyes and shuddered. "You were right. He wouldn't have wanted to live like that. I should thank you, but I don't think I can. I still want to bring him home."

"I get it," I said. I didn't want her thanks, anyway. That would be awkward. "Don't worry about tit."

"Fine," she said almost too quickly. "We have to think about Mink now, anyway. Come on back to my house and we can plan our next steps."

Riga called over the server, and to my surprise, bought my breakfast. I guess she wasn't all that bad, after all.

13

Riga stared at me intently. "We should go. I'll get you to the airport. Don't even bother to check out of the hotel. Leave your stuff and just get out."

I shook my head. "Not going."

Riga caught my gaze and kept it. "Go."

"Even Ware doesn't get me to do what he wants by ordering me," I said. "Actually, he rarely gets me to do what he wants, no matter how he behaves. However, I bet even he wouldn't try to convince me to leave Brooklyn alone with Mink."

Riga took a few moments to consider and frowned, but nodded toward the door. "Fine. I'll try to convince you again later. But if you're determined to stay, then for now, you should come to my house. I have something to show you."

I got up and left the restaurant. Riga went to the counter to pay. She joined me at the car less than a minute later and I climbed in.

Riga drove north, past St. John's Pass and Indian Shores. She turned eastward and took some smaller roads until she turned onto a small street with somewhat tired-looking houses. Riga piloted the car into the driveway of a small yellow house on a gravel lot. The yard was mostly bereft of life except for a huge live oak.

The day was heating up but Riga's house either had no air conditioning or she wasn't using it. She pointed me at a small kitchen table in her tiny bright yellow kitchen. "Sit. I'll fetch it."

I sat, wondering how long it would be before she either attacked me, or I died of heat prostration. All the windows I could see were tightly closed. No air conditioning and the house buttoned up tight. My guess was that Riga spent little time here. No need to run up the electric bill if you weren't going to take advantage of the cool air it bought.

The woman returned with what appeared to be a scrapbook. She placed it in front of me and then sat down.

"Coffee?"

"No thanks," I said. "It's a bit close in here, don't you think? Especially for drinking hot liquids."

"Once my husband died, there wasn't much reason to stick around," she said, her voice distant. "I was spending a lot of time at the park, working out his habits. Figuring out how to catch him, bring him home."

"I still can't believe you thought you could succeed at that."

"Then you've never lost anyone close to you."

My heart clenched and my gut went cold. I blinked back tears again, but this time, they threatened to escape my eyes. My throat closed up. I wanted to cuss at Riga, maybe yell at her about Castro. About how I'd killed the man I loved. But my throat was so tight, I knew I wouldn't be able to say a thing.

The loss bit deeply still, but at the same time, there was something dark between me and the grief. Something alien. I should be grateful I didn't feel the full force of Castro's loss, I supposed. But the fact that the darkness was who she was, and that she wasn't going to let go without a fight, was not comforting.

"Oh," said Riga.

I looked at her. She had a strange "I just sucked on a lemon" look on her face.

"Yeah," I said. "I did lose someone close. And the Queen Bitch was the one who made sure I was the one who killed him."

Riga didn't even flinch at that, but I suppose nothing to do with the Forlorn could surprise her too much. Not after watching her husband turn into a hungry, grasping supernatural killing machine.

She pointed at the book she'd brought. "Take a look."

I flipped the scrapbook open. The first few pages held newspaper clippings from the 1990s. One was about the opening of the Angels' Share in 1992. "I guess that's when Ware moved to town," I said softly.

"As far as I know," she said. "He never gave me many details but I'm pretty sure before that he'd been in D.C. And before that, either Sacramento or maybe Saskatchewan. He'd drop a few city names but it wasn't generally clear to me if he'd stayed any length of time in them, or in what order he'd lived in them if he had actually spent time there. Once in a while, he'd mention other cities. Rome. Byzantium. Timbuktu. Great Zimbabwe. Ur. I tried to glean any information I could, but he didn't let out a lot of information."

"That hasn't changed. I can barely get him to tell me anything, even when he knows I need to know something. It's like he's too used to keeping things to himself, he can't even let information go when he knows he should."

"I don't miss that," said Riga. "Keep going."

After the newspaper clippings were pages of notes taken on the back of bar napkins, pieces of notepad paper, even written in the margins of torn bits of newspaper.

Wednesday, the new guy stopped in again. Reddish hair, drinks all evening. Looks homeless, but it's clear he's one of THEM.

Well, she'd met Fish, then. "Fish," said. "I think he's in the sinkhole Zireya took over."

"Really? He seemed pretty pathetic to me. Not likely to cause any trouble. What did he do to get Ware to dump him in a sinkhole?"

"He got his wings back and went on a killing spree."

Riga's mouth opened, then shut without a sound. Guess I'd finally found something to surprise her with.

"I fought him, injured him. Last I saw of him, he was trapped in some kind of in-between state, looking partly human, and partly like one of them the way they used to look. When they lived in space as weird crystalline creatures. It didn't look like a pleasant form to be trapped in. Pieces of him shifted from one form to another constantly. It was disturbing to watch. Probably even more to experience firsthand."

"God in heaven," said Riga softly. "Even one of their own...I thought Ware didn't necessarily have that level of cruelty in him. I guess they're all bastards."

I shrugged. "Oh, I've no doubt he can be cruel. But I don't know that Fish's condition was something he could do much about. Keeping him from killing humans might have been the best Ware could do for now."

I flipped through the book some more. More notes.

The scary guy is back but Ware kicked him out. Said he had nothing to say to him.

Lucy brought in a cat and dumped it on the bar. Gina took it home when Ware said Lucy would probably just kill it later if it were still here. She hates cats, apparently. Why did she bring it in? My only guess is casual cruelty. To the cat, or Gina, or both?

The one with the scarred ear was outside, but he didn't come in. I'm glad. I get so scared when he's around.

Gina quit, or something. No one's seen her in days. Ware says she moved away from STL. I think he's lying. Something happened to her. What happened? Which one of them did it? The scarred guy?

*Lucy? Something happened to the cat so my money's on Lucy. I hate
her even more than I'm afraid of her.*

*Little Girl was in again, saying crazy things about thunder.
Ware told her to shut up. She did. She always does what he says. He
told her "No more riding horses." I don't know what that means but
it's clearly a euphemism.*

God. Riga had overheard a lot. I closed my eyes. The
Thunderer had been born, I'd heard. Oya—Little Girl—had left me
a note saying he was born and Mia was dead. Lucy killed her. More
sins to chalk up on Lucy's account. I can't believe that, not so long
ago, I'd actually thought she might be nice and, compared to the
others, relatively harmless.

"Riding horses is what Oya means when she possesses people.
Like in *The Exorcist*. She can only possess people like us, though.
The Lost. I guess it's a consequence of Zireya's genetic legacy."

"Oya?"

"Little Girl. I couldn't call her that, so she said I could call her
Babs. That didn't seem to fit, either, so the next option she
provided was Oya. That's worked for me."

"Hmm," said Riga. "Babs. So she thinks she's Saint Barbara or
something?"

"I have no idea who that is, but I wouldn't put it past her. I
think these creatures have been posing as prophets, leaders, gods,
and whatever else, for thousands of years. Being a saint would be
par for the course."

Riga snorted; apparently, she had already reached this
conclusion. Not surprising, since she'd known Ware and his
compatriots much longer than I'd known him.

I closed the book. "Look, this is all interesting, but I don't see
how it's going to help us or Brooklyn. We need to get around Mink
somehow."

"What about the other one last night? I didn't know him."

"Aditya. Ware calls him The Musician. He's tricky. He opposed me in London; wanted to keep Ware from getting Zireya's tooth as a talisman. He can drag a human's astral form out of their body and take them to some kind of spiritual dimension where he is in control. He did that to me and attacked me there, but I got my hands on his flute and jammed it into his skull. I got away. So he's not averse to being violent, but then, he was also as good as his word. When he said he'd leave me and Brooklyn alone until dawn, he followed through. His flute has some kind of power, but I don't know what it is or how to use it. His real name is something like Music Enduring Through Time."

"His name?"

"They all have these elaborate names. Too long to remember. Ware's is shorter; he's the Lightbearer. Maybe because his wings were so white."

"White wings?" Riga shook her head. "You've found out more than I ever did. But the Lightbearer? I can believe that one. Things you *bear* are generally burdens, and Ware always seemed burdened."

"Huh. Odd that light is a burden. Wouldn't darkness be more of a burden?"

Riga shrugged. "Oh, I don't know. Ignorance can be a heavy burden but knowledge even more so. The old chestnut is *blissful ignorance*, not *blissful knowledge*."

"That's nice," I said. "But what do we do now to rescue Brooklyn?"

"You won't leave town?"

"No."

Riga's shoulders slumped. "I had hoped not to have to show you this. Follow me."

She got up from the table, suddenly moving as if she'd aged twenty years in the past five seconds. I got up, wondering if this was the right move. Maybe I should just get out.

But my gut told me I'd better see what Riga wanted to show me. She went to a door at the end of a short hall. "I'd have done this in the basement, if houses in Florida had basements," she said. "I had to make do and hope for the best."

She turned the doorknob with a trembling hand and swung the door open. Then she stood back and let me look in.

The single window had been boarded up. Padding had been attached to all the walls. Overhead, a single bulb burnt with a sickly yellow light.

But what stood out were the chains. Chains attached to each wall. Chains coming down from the ceiling. Chains piled up in the corner.

"I was going to keep him here," Riga said slowly. I could barely hear her over the pounding in my chest. "My husband. A Rake."

I didn't know what to say. Hearing her say she'd planned to keep her husband around after he'd been turned into a Rake had been shocking enough. But seeing the chains...that was something else entirely. That made it real. My stomach turned and I felt like I needed to puke up my breakfast.

"How is this going to help?" I said around the nausea.

"Not the chains. I don't think we can just lock up Mink. Or Isya, should he get out." She pointed toward the corner to my right. "Those. That's what might help."

I looked over. Some oddly shaped rods sat in a small pile on the ugly avocado green threadbare carpet.

"Yeah? What are those?"

Riga took a deep sigh before saying, "Cattle prods. I thought I'd be able to keep him from escaping if he learned to fear them enough."

"And you think we can use them on Mink?"

"Why not? I know we can't kill them, but surely we can hurt them."

Somehow, I doubted cattle prods would do more than tickle Mink, but what did I know? I walked into the room and picked up one of the cattle prods. "Easy to use, I guess."

"Turn them on and shock whatever you touch with the nasty end," she said.

"Great. Let's put them in the car, and then see if we can round up our best bet."

"What's that?"

"The guy with the magic flute."

14

"Are you sure we can trust him?"

"I think we can trust his word, so first we have to figure out how to find him, ask if he'll help us, and go from there. If he says no, then we may have two Forlorn against us. If he says yes, then we should be able to trust him."

"Not ideal," said Riga. "But then, what is? So, where do we find him?"

I grabbed a couple of the cattle prods and walked back toward the kitchen, noticing this time how bare Riga's house was. A tattered gold couch sat near the front door. Curtains hung raggedly over windows with cracked frames. The carpet had seen better days, and those days had clearly been decades ago. An empty bookshelf sat in a second bedroom to my left while a third bedroom to my right sported a small bed and one chest-of-drawers whose drawers seemed too warped to fit into their old spaces. Two of them sat strangely crookedly and obviously no longer could be pushed in.

"This sort of dungeon is normally in the basement."

"No basements here," said Riga. "Unless you want a swimming pool under your house. My house is seven feet above sea level. Most around here aren't even at that level."

"Hmm," I said. That made sense, though I'd lived in the Midwest my entire life, so a land without basements underneath the houses seemed freakishly alien. At least as alien as palm trees, warm aqua-colored ocean waves, and sand everywhere.

"I've sold everything I could sell," said Riga. "For the soundproofing, chains, cattle prods. All that stuff. Making a dungeon in your house isn't the cheapest kind of renovation. At least I'm in a house and not a mobile home or condo or apartment. My neighbors aren't far, but they're not right on the other side of a thin wall."

"Got it."

"Go on out to the car and think about where we need to go," said Riga. "I've got to get my purse."

"Sure." I exited the house by the back door and walked to the car. Riga followed only a few moments later, her purse hanging awkwardly over one shoulder.

"Where do we go first?" she asked as we got in the car. The interior was the temperature of hell, and the air conditioner made very little dent in the unpleasantness of it all. That was Florida in the summer, I guess. I would never be moving here.

"I'm not sure. Start driving back toward the museum, and I'll see if I can sense anything. I don't know that I'll be able to, but it's worth a shot. As long as the Queen Bitch has her fingers in my brain, let's use her."

"Sounds good."

I let Riga pick the direction and just let my thoughts go. At some point, she pulled over to a gas station and filled up the car. I got out into the heat and walked to the main street. I ignored the cars because the flowering bushes were much more enticing. I had no idea what they were; the bushes sported tons of pink and white flowers. But pink and white *what* was a mystery. Didn't matter. I just enjoyed the beauty. St. Louis had its good parts but an abundance of flowering bushes along the roads was not one of them.

Something tickled the back of my mind. I stood stock still, wondering if the feeling was coming from down the road. Or maybe from behind me? I couldn't tell. Just because it felt like it was in the back of my head didn't mean it was in that direction. For some reason, the road ahead was what captured my interest.

I don't know how long I stood there, but at some point, I realized Riga had pulled the car alongside me. We were out of the way enough that the rest of the gas station traffic could get around us so I had no idea how long she'd stayed there. She had no reason to hurry me.

"I, uh, think we should go this way," I said, gesturing down the road.

"Okay," she said. "I would have gone that way anyway. The museum's in that direction."

"Oh." Trust me senses to be taking me back to the museum and not to Aditya. Well, maybe he was *at* the museum. A two-fer.

I wiped my forehead. I'd gotten quite sweaty while standing out in the sun staring down the street. Now all I wanted was a shower. And some a/c. And a cold drink.

And a new life.

I got back in the car and Riga handed me a bottle of water. "I needed some," she said. "Figured you would, too."

I jacked the car's a/c as high as it would go. That was two of the four things I'd wished for. The new life would have made me much happier, though.

Can't have everything, I suppose. The shower I could probably get later. The new life wasn't in the cards.

As we traveled closer to our destination, I noticed some birds on the horizon. They were high overhead and had deeply forked tails. "What are those?"

Riga saw where I was looking and said, "Magnificent frigatebirds. Usually, you only see one at a time. I've never seen a whole group of them like that."

"Are they over the museum?" I asked with some trepidation. Because, of course they would be. Why not? All alien weirdness needed to amass in a central location, right?

"Mmm, I don't know," she said cautiously. "I don't think they're far enough south. Maybe something else is going on."

As we approached the circling birds, it became clear they weren't quite where we were headed. In fact, they were hanging out over a rather large condo complex behind a privacy gate.

"We don't have a code," said Riga. "We can't get in."

I just glanced at her briefly, wondering if we'd even need one. There had to be an upside to Queen Bitch being in my head, right? "Wait here," I said.

I got out of the car and walked to the gate. A small box with a ten-key pad sat next to the gate. I lifted my hand and let my fingers do the walking. Four numbers and the green button.

Bzzt. The gate opened. I got back in the car and Riga drove on through. "I recorded that on my phone," she said. "So we'll know the number next time."

"Next time? I'm hoping we get Brooklyn back and I get to leave this fucking town, like, this evening. Morning at the latest."

"Better to have and not need," said Riga. "Now, which condo are we going to?"

"I don't know, of course. Find somewhere to park and I guess I'll just meander through these lovely grounds."

Actually, the grounds *were* exceedingly lovely. I was instantly jealous that anyone could live in a place where the buildings looked bright and new, the plants all bloomed beautiful white, pink, and orange flowers, and the sidewalks were made to look like cobblestones. Massive trees shaded the lawns and many different kinds of birds strutted around looking through the landscaped grass and the bushes, I assumed for their lunch.

True that the weather here did not tempt me to move, but the beauty of the location almost made up for the heat.

Almost.

Didn't matter anyway. I'd be lucky to live long enough to make it to thirty. I wouldn't ever be moving to someplace as lovely—and expensive—as this.

As I passed one of the buildings, I spotted a pool in the distance. Several people floated in the pool while others laid in the chaise chairs around the perimeter.

One of the men in the pool had long black hair and lovely cinnamon skin. Aditya.

I walked up to the fence surrounding the pool. "Hey, Musician," I called out.

He turned and smiled at me. "Teryl. I thought I might be harder to find, but I see that was a fool's hope."

"As long as your ex-queen takes an interest in my life, I doubt any of you will be able to truly get away from me. Not for long, anyway."

He shrugged and got out of the pool. He sauntered over to the fence and sat down in a white plastic chair. "What can I do for you, then?"

"I want to get Brooklyn back. Mink has her. You know Brooklyn has nothing to do with this."

Aditya gave me some serious side-eye. "As long as she's helping you, she's involved. You can hardly say she has *nothing to do with this*."

"Driving me around hardly seems a sin worth threatening death over. Mink made it clear she doesn't care if Brooklyn lives or dies, and I do care, so guess who's going to pay?"

The Forlorn took a deep sigh. "I certainly believe you'll try to make her pay. But Mink isn't a pushover. Not like me."

"I seem to recall you capturing me and forcing me into an astral dimension controlled by you. Not exactly a pushover."

"I seem to recall you harming me with my own flute in that very same dimension. Not exactly impressive on my part, to permit the person I kidnapped into the dimension to injure me badly enough they were able to leave without my permission."

He had a point. Still, I wasn't exactly well-disposed toward him and his ever-cheery demeanor. "Whatever. Tell me anything I can use to get Brooklyn away from Mink."

"You want my advice?"

"Want? No, not really. Need? Probably."

"Why don't you just call Ware? He can tell you anything you want to know about Mink."

The look on my face apparently got through to him. Before I could say something like *I'd sooner eat a live goldfish than talk to him*, Aditya said, "Ah. Well, you'll have to put your grievances aside at some point. Just not today, I guess."

"Not today. Not tomorrow. Now, tell me about Mink. How do I beat her?"

He glanced around and gestured toward a bench under a tree a short distance away. "Look. I'll grab a towel and my shirt and join you on that bench in a few seconds, okay?"

"Fine."

I went over to the bench and sat down. A lazy salt breeze slid by, which was far more relaxing than it had any right to be. Riga sat down on a nearby bench. She nodded to me, almost as if we were spies and she was keeping an eye on some kind of clandestine meeting where I'd be exchanging nuclear secrets or something.

True to his word, Aditya came over, paisley shirt unbuttoned and bright red towel wrapped around his waist. His hair tumbled down his shoulders and chest. I had to hand it to him; he was like a piece of art.

A dangerous alien piece of art.

He sat down and leaned back against the back of the bench. "All right. Keep in mind, Mink can make sinkholes like Ware. He's more powerful; I don't doubt he can make better ones, or a greater quantity with less effort. But she can do it, too. And if she can make them, she can probably find them and open them, too. Even if they're not hers."

"How much of that is guesswork?"

"I could be wrong, but probably. I'm sure Ware can do it to any sinkhole, but Mink can probably do it to the sinkholes of others. A long time ago there was another one of us who could make sinkholes. He went by Nebulae and Stars Prostrate Themselves Before Me. Kind of a narcissistic ass, actually."

"The name kind of gives it away."

"Yes. I'm not sure he ever picked a nice short human name. I called him Prostrating Stars for short. I don't think he cared for it. Haven't seen him for ages. Like, literally thousands of years. Maybe he retired to a sinkhole and is just sitting there twiddling his thumbs. Anyway, he could make them. It took a lot out of him; he was never as talented as Mink or Ware. He would never have been able to open one of theirs, either."

"So why did he think he was so great, then? Sounds like overcompensation."

Aditya chuckled. "Maybe. His great skill was that he could affect the weather. You wanted rain to put out a forest fire? Call him. You want a tornado to wipe away your enemies? He was your guy. None of us had control of the weather like he did. So maybe he wasn't completely overcompensating with the name."

"Does that mean he was like the Thunderer?"

Aditya blinked. "What?"

"I know Oya was trying to engineer the birth of something called the Thunderer. Sounds like someone who could change the weather. It rained pretty much for the entirety of Mia's last trimester."

Aditya shook his head. "I don't know what the Thunderer is capable of. Maybe anything. The prophecies aren't clear. Anyway, Mink can make sinkholes. Otherwise, she doesn't have a lot of powers. Not like Zireya, who really could do everything, or Ware, who can do most things. Isya, too. Except neither Ware nor Isya was very good at music. And Mink literally can't even hold a tune. For musical talent, if you don't come to me, you'd have to go to Lucy or maybe Yama."

"I don't need musical talent. I need a way to get Brooklyn away from Mink. Sounds like, as long as she isn't making a sinkhole, she's not that dangerous."

"Well, except for of course we're stronger than regular humans, and pretty much invulnerable. You want to hurt her, you're going to need a talisman."

"Like what? Ware had most of them, I think. Stored in that sinkhole of his that Zireya commandeered. But even if she wanted me to have whatever was inside, it's in St. Louis."

"It is *now*. But you're here, and therefore, in some metaphysical sense, so is she."

"Mm-hmm. And?"

"And I just told you. Zireya could do *anything*. You want something from that sinkhole, then get it. Especially if it's something she wants you to have. Nothing could get in your way. Not Mink. Not me. Certainly not Ware."

I sat back and thought about that. I could do *anything*? Provided Zireya wanted me to be able to do it? That was one of the scariest things I'd ever heard. No one, not even an alien bitch, should be able to do *anything*.

"Fine," I said. "I can do all kinds of cool shit that I don't even know or have time to research and learn. I mean, how do I do any of this? How do you exercise your powers?"

He shook his head. "They are intrinsic to who we are. I can do what I do without thinking. By instinct."

"In case you haven't realized it, this isn't instinct for me."

"Yes, I know. But it means I don't know what to tell you. Zireya's power, at least a shred of it, is inside you. Use it. That's all I can advise you."

I closed my eyes and clutched my hands into fists. Why couldn't someone have written up a nice owner's manual for when you're at least partially possessed by a distant dead alien ancestress. You know, helpful tips, in alphabetical order. With a Table of Contents and an index and everything.

I opened my eyes. Riga sat rigidly where she had been sitting moments before. Aditya, however, was gone.

15

"Are you sure we can trust him?"

That was at least the second time Riga had asked since we'd left the condo complex, and the third time today. Or maybe the fourth. I was going to stop counting.

"He may not be a friend, but he seems to take some pride in being honest. I'm not sure what he would gain by telling me Mink could open sinkholes if she can't."

Riga shook her head. "That's not what I mean. I mean, he told you Zireya could do anything, right? Anything? What if you start to believe that? You're just her descendant. *You* can't do anything. Why would he want to put that idea in your head?"

"That doesn't make it a lie."

"I didn't say he lied. I asked if you could trust him. That's different."

She had a point. I didn't answer and just watched the strip malls and public parking lots go by. The rest of St. Petersburg seemed to be out and about on this fine sunny day, carrying towels and chairs to the beaches, buying ice cream cones, and having a good time with friends and family.

A stab of jealousy made my heart pump hard for a few seconds. Why couldn't I have that life? It should be me and Castro being happy at a vacation location we'd always wanted to experience. Castro had always said he wanted to see Colorado. We'd never seriously planned a trip but I'd assumed we'd get out there someday. I'd had visions of the two of us walking a trail surrounded by mountain peaks and evergreens. Maybe we'd sit by a mountain lake and watch lazy clouds pass by overhead. If we were lucky, maybe we'd spot a bighorn sheep or a mountain bluebird. Instead, I was here in Florida, suffering under the heat, and Castro was dead and in the ground.

Soon enough, I began to recognize the surroundings. I hadn't been paying too much attention, but a big pink hotel was a bit hard to miss. It had to be the biggest building in the area.

After the pink monstrosity, the area turned more residential. Large homes shaded by tall palm trees sat quietly on narrow streets, bracketing smaller, older homes that looked tired and weathered. I had no doubt that the moment those owners sold the tired houses, the new owners would knock down the old building and put up one of the modern new two-story behemoths. Because who didn't need a 3000 square foot home when you lived near a beach?

Eventually, Riga turned right and immediately pulled into an empty spot on the road. "Gotta take parking where you find it," she said. "We can walk the rest of the way."

I got out of the car and followed Riga down the street. She clutched her purse tightly to her side and strode stiffly down the street and around a corner. I followed a bit more slowly, trying to notice anything unusual. If Mink had Brooklyn here, would they simply be standing around on the sidewalk? I suspected Mink would make things a tiny bit more difficult. I was tempted to tell Riga to slow down, keep an eye on our surroundings. But then, would that actually help? It wasn't like Mink wasn't expecting us. Here we were, in broad daylight, arriving as she had demanded. How much use would caution really be?

The closer we got to the museum, the darker the day seemed to get. Surely that was just me. But I had a way to check.

"So, is the area getting darker to you? Cloudier maybe? Foggy?"

Riga glanced back at me. "It's bright and sunny. Just like it was a minute ago. Why?"

I gestured vaguely around, as if trying to indicate the entirety of the neighborhood. "It's like there's a shadow over everything. It's a lot worse than yesterday. Before, it just seemed to hover over the area, and it wasn't so dark. It was more of a feeling of darkness, and only a hint of an actual real shadow. Now it's everywhere and it's something my eyes are picking up on, to the point where it's like a curtain in my way. Something between me and the world."

Riga frowned. "But you can still see, right? It's not so dark you're blinded."

"Blinded? No. Well, not yet, anyway."

We walked a couple more minutes until we stood in front of the museum. I glanced around but didn't see anything odd in this oddly gray world. Well, the small white birds strutting around the park across the street seemed a bit odd to me; they had curved beaks and ice blue eyes. Very striking, and a little creepy.

"We're early. Let's go over to The Hurricane," said Riga. "We can see if there's a table where we can watch the museum. Keep an eye on things."

"A stake-out. Sure, why not?"

We walked across the street, the park, and the other half of the street to the main entrance to the restaurant. A smiling hostess showed us to a table on the side of the restaurant closest to the museum. She seemed a little confused that we didn't want to sit outside or on the roof, but she recovered quickly and left us with our menus.

Riga opened the menu almost with reverence. When our server came by, Riga ordered water and added, "I need to look over this for a few minutes more."

"Sure. And you?" the server asked me.

"Me? Oh, water's fine."

The server left. I glanced over the menu; the food was more expensive than home and some of it was a mystery to me. What could Seashore Tots be? Truffle fries?

"I think I'll have scallops," said Riga. She seemed sad. I guessed she was thinking to days past where she'd come here with her husband. Maybe scallops had been their shared appetizer or something. Castro and I had liked to go to bars and get fried green beans to share. We couldn't be the only couple who ever did that.

Thinking of Castro of course sent another stab of grief around my gut and up through my heart, nearly choking me. Riga's grief had to be at least as raw, if not more. After all, her husband hadn't just died, he'd turned into a monster.

A monster she'd planned to keep in a bedroom. In chains. Controlled with cattle prods.

Riga's life might be one of the few more messed up than mine.

I had no idea what to get. I glanced at Riga helplessly. "I don't even know what half this stuff might be. And, besides, *alligator bites*? Do people really eat alligator?"

"Yes," she said without humor. "All the time. They're a bit rubbery here, though. I'd recommend the crab cakes."

"Not the scallops?"

"You could certainly try them. I think they're excellent but they're often an acquired taste."

"No time like the present to acquire a new habit. Why not scallops?"

The server returned. Riga's expression turned into something I couldn't identify. It wasn't grief or regret. At least, I thought it wasn't. But then, what *was* it?

None of my business.

"Scallops, blackened, with Korean BBQ sauce," she said. "And for my friend, jerk scallops with citrus sauce. Oh, and some alligator bites and crab cakes."

"Sure thing. Anything else?"

"Sure. Key lime pie and a tequila sunrise. You want any dessert or anything else to drink?"

"No," I said, wondering how Riga thought the two of us could make it through four appetizers, let alone dessert.

Plus, alcohol was probably a bad idea.

What the hell. This whole trip was one bad idea after another. "Sure, okay, a double shot of a Glenlivet twelve year."

"I don't think we have that," said the server.

Not surprising. You couldn't ask a beachfront restaurant to have the inventory of a bar. I'd try a variety then. "Four Roses? Tullamore Dew?" When the server didn't react right away, I settled for an old standard. "Jack?"

"We have Jack." The server's smile returned.

"Fine. A double of Jack. Neat."

I couldn't complain about the service. Or the food. Our order arrived fairly promptly and I nibbled on scallops, crab cakes, and alligator. Riga ate it with a kind of quiet enjoyment that seemed a bit out of character, and a bit odd. After all, she could always come back here whenever she liked. I doubt alligator or crab or scallops were coming off the menu anytime soon.

I kept my eye on the park and the museum on the other side. Long past the time when our appetizers had been eaten and Riga had slowly appreciated her key lime pie small bite by small bite, we were still watching. I'd ordered more Jack but Riga had settled for more water.

I had no idea what the bill might be but the server definitely deserved a huge tip since we were squatting at one of her tables for most of the afternoon.

Finally, Riga sighed. "I guess they'll get here eventually." She put down several large bills on the table, certainly enough to cover the food and a ridiculously large tip. Our server should be pleased.

We left the restaurant and went to the park.

"Maybe you should try what Aditya suggested," said Riga hesitantly. "Before they get here. I should have suggested it before we went to the Hurricane, perhaps. Now you've had quite a bit to drink, so maybe it won't work."

"Four Jacks over three hours on top of food aren't going to be a problem," I said. "But what is it you want me to try?"

"Aditya said you'd need a talisman. You said they were in Ware's sinkhole. Can you retrieve them from here?"

That seemed crazy. "I've only been in that sinkhole once. Ware put me in, Zireya kicked me out. I don't know what you want me to do."

"Well, I don't know, either," she said with some exasperation. "Just try. Can you sense anything at all?"

I had nothing else to do, so why not?

I stood still and closed my eyes. I imagined being on the bridge, just prior to jumping into the abyss below. By all rights, I should land in the Mississippi River. But I knew instead I would end up in Ware's sinkhole.

The sinkhole opened and I felt it. Deep in my gut, I *felt* it. It was like a tickling in my abdomen. The tickling snaked out to my feet and my shoulders but was definitely rooted deep in my body.

I stretched my senses as much as I knew how, but the feeling didn't change. It was just a feeling, and after maybe thirty seconds or so, it faded away.

"Well?" asked Riga as I opened my eyes. "What happened?"

"Nothing. Well, I felt something but it went away fairly quickly. I'm not sure if the feeling was even something real, or if it were something I conjured up just because I wanted to feel something. Power of suggestion and all that."

Riga frowned. "Well, try again! You need to know if you have any of Zireya's powers. You need to know how to use them."

"Why? Why do I have to do anything?"

"You want your friend back!" At this point, Riga was yelling.

She had a point, but I'd lost interest in listening to her. "You know what? Forget this," I said. "I do want Brooklyn back, and I'm going to get her back. But I don't need you, and I don't need the bitch who wants my mind under her control. You, Zireya, Ware—everyone wants something from me. But none of you want to provide something in return. I'm just supposed to do what you want when you want it because it'll, somehow, help something undefined. I've had enough!"

Riga's face flushed red. "You have no idea what I'm ready to do to *provide something in return*. You have no idea."

"Maybe I don't want to know," I said, wishing I could just leave this woman behind. But she was right about Brooklyn. I couldn't leave her to Mink's tender ministrations. Mink had no reason to keep her alive if I didn't cooperate with helping Mink find and open the sinkhole in the museum.

Riga fell silent, though her face remained flushed. I stared at her while she clamped her lips shut. Her eyes blinked quickly as if she were trying to push back tears, but surely that was anger and not sadness written across her face.

"Finally," said a familiar voice. "The gang's all here."

I turned to see Aditya on a bench, holding a fruity drink sporting a little umbrella. He gestured toward the museum with the drink. I glanced over and saw Brooklyn standing on the sidewalk in front of the building. Her gaze was blank and her arms hung limply at her sides. It was as if she were in some kind of trance.

Well, maybe she was.

I darted forward, just as Mink stepped out of a car and stood between me and Brooklyn.

"Hello," she said brightly as she blocked my path. "Time to give me what I want."

16

I stopped in the middle of the street. Traffic was light enough that I had no worries about being run over, at least for a minute or two.

Mink's expression was friendly but that didn't fool me. She was going to do whatever she felt necessary to get what she wanted, and being friendly was only a diversion. She wore a white sundress which showed off her toned shoulders and tanned skin. Looking at her, anyone would suspect she was local, and not an immortal alien creature bent on releasing her megalomaniacal leader out of his supernatural prison.

"I don't know how to do what you want," I said without preamble.

Mink's smile didn't falter. She glanced to my left and nodded; I assume she'd spotted Riga. Or Aditya. Or both.

"I don't think you consciously know how to do what I want, but it's clear Zireya's taken an interest in you." Her attention was back on me now. Her sweet heart-shaped face framed in auburn hair was as pretty as could be. If I didn't know better, I'd be tempted to trust her. But I knew better. She was as much as bitch as Zireya, just not as powerful. "That's been obvious for a while, even if Ware was in denial. Zireya knows what I want. Nothing was too difficult for her. Just give her free rein and she can get Isya out of that sinkhole."

"She sounds like a real diva," I said. "Knows everything, bullies everyone. But beautiful enough no one seriously opposes her. Honestly, I had no idea that aliens had mean girls just like we do."

Mink just smiled wider. "You are so funny, you know that? Something Zireya never was. She was always so serious, so pretentious. Eons ago, I thought she encompassed everything. But coming to this tiny little rock and taking human form made me realize she didn't know about humor. So she had at least one failing."

"That's nice," I said. "Good for you. You get a cookie. Now, let me have Brooklyn."

"No," said Mink with a backward glance toward my friend. "Only once Isya is free."

"You don't even know he's here."

Mink took a deep breath. "You know we live forever, right? I've had *oodles* of time to figure out which of Ware's sinkholes was the right one. This one is it."

"Because it moves around?"

Mink shrugged. "That. Plus, it has a different feel. I'd call it a song, but it's not really that. You don't have a word for it. It's like each sinkhole hums in a unique way that gives away something about it. This one holds Isya."

Maybe she could really figure out which sinkhole had her boss in it by listening to them hum or sing or whatever. Maybe she was as clever as she thought she was.

"But what if you're wrong?" I asked because, *what if.* "Say I open it and he's not there. I still want you to release Brooklyn."

"Oh, you can have her once the thing is open," Mink said off-handedly. "It's not like she's any use to me after that. But I'm not wrong."

Something in my mind agreed with her. Fucking bitch in my head thought this was the sinkhole with Isya, too.

Suddenly, Mink got even more interested in me. "Oh, is Zireya poking you in the brain, dear? I bet that's not so comfortable."

"Whatever." I walked around her and went up to Brooklyn, who still stood staring blankly ahead. "Brooklyn?"

Her expression did not change, though I thought I caught a glimpse of terror in her eyes before it slid away and left nothing in its place. Anger bubbled up in my chest and burned behind my eyelids.

"She didn't do anything to you," I said. "You should let her go."

"She didn't do anything? She's helping you, and you're helping Ware. By the transitive property, that means she's as deep into this as you are."

I turned around. Mink was still smiling. She made a "shoo" gesture. "Now go to the sinkhole. I don't think you have to go inside the building, though, which is good, since we'd have to break in. Go behind."

I put a hand on Brooklyn's shoulder. "Don't worry. I'll get you out of this." I walked toward the museum, my steps crunching on the gravel-and-shell of what would constitute, at home, a *yard*. Here, I'm not sure what I'd call it. Ugly, for sure.

Practical, I suppose. You certainly wouldn't have to mow it.

The tickle in my gut began migrating toward my left kidney. The sensation was so weird I had to stop walking and I clutched at my stomach with my hands.

So, so weird. Not painful, not quite. But hardly a comfortable feeling.

"What is it? Keep going," said Mink.

"I think it moved," I said. I gestured toward my left. "Over there somewhere."

Indeed, the darkness that had blanketed the street earlier had shifted. The street was still darker than it should be, but now the darkness was centered elsewhere.

"It moved?"

Mink strode forward, head cocked slightly, lips pursed. She frowned and spun around slowly, as if she were the needle on a compass and had to keep moving until she found north.

"I think you're right," she said at last. "This way." She took off toward the beach.

We crossed the street and walked past the Paradise Grille and onto the beach. Beachgoers waded in the placid water or sat on beach towels. Several children equipped with plastic shovels and pails dug holes in the sand. None paid attention to us.

Though Mink was in front, following her own senses, my new sinkhole-finding gut-sense indicated she was on the right trail. We walked on the powdery white sand for a few hundred feet before Mink stopped and pointed to a spot slightly to her right and in front. "Here. It's here."

I was happy enough to stop. Walking on soft sand was a lot harder than it looked, and a lot of sand had migrated into my shoes. I was beginning to hate the beach.

"Now, open it," she said.

"Why don't you do it?" I asked. "Sincerely, I'm asking. Okay, I'm also being sarcastic, but on top of that, I don't know why you can't open it when you can sense it and follow it."

"So can you."

"Not me. *Her*. And not before just now."

"Just open it."

I had no way to know how to do that, but I had to think of Brooklyn. I stepped toward the spot Mink had indicated. My gut-sense tingled some more. Why couldn't this be more like some little tickle on the end of my nose, or something more acceptable like that? Instead, I felt as if my intestines were slowly tying themselves into knots—real knots—and trying to escape my body.

It was not a nice feeling.

I closed my eyes and tried to sense something. Anything. How was I supposed to do this?

I don't know how much time passed. One minute? Two?

"Come on," said Mink. "Do you think I have until the end of time?"

"Actually, I think you do," I said.

"Well, Brooklyn certainly doesn't. If you don't get this open right now, I'll take something from her."

My heart sank. "Something?"

"A body part is too obvious. But what about her personality? Or I could trap her in her brain. She could be perfectly fine mentally but paralyzed physically. Locked-In Syndrome. That's gotta be fun."

I swallowed heavily, stress making me sweat far more than the fading heat of the day. I turned back toward the Paradise Grille. Brooklyn stood about twenty feet away, still staring blankly.

Mink was in between us, and was no longer smiling. The unpleasant frown and the flash of anger in her eyes chilled me. I involuntarily took a step back. The Forlorn could get fucking scary when they wanted. Mink might look like a demure little thing most of the time, but she was no empty-headed pretty young woman.

She was dangerous.

Mink raised a hand toward Brooklyn, who began moaning and swaying on her feet. Her face changed from passive and blank to pained. White pain lines formed around her mouth, and she tossed her head to the side over and over while working her jaw as if trying to scream but being restrained.

"It can take a while," said Mink evenly. "But in the end, she'll be trapped forever in her own head."

"Stop! Stop it!"

Mink glanced toward me and winked. "Then just open the sinkhole. That's all it will take."

Brooklyn's moaning became quieter but more intense. She began shaking.

"Not sure how much more she can take," said Mink conversationally.

I gritted my teeth and closed my eyes The damn sinkhole was here but how was I supposed to just *know* what to do about it?

It seemed everyone knew more about this than I did. The frustration built in my body so much that I was shaking, too. *What do I do?* I screamed into my mind.

Immediately, the presence in my mind grew sharper, painful. I bit back a moan and dropped to my knees. In my head, I felt as if my mind reached out beyond the physical limits of my body. I reached out to the sinkhole in St. Louis, the one Zireya now had control of. Inside it was her body and all the talismans Ware had collected over the centuries.

And suddenly, the knowledge was *there*. I could use this tendril of my mind to reach out for the sinkhole. It was mine. I controlled it. Ware had no claim on it.

In my head, I pictured it as a satchel. I picked it up by its metaphorical handle and clutched it to me. And it was here. In Florida.

How should it have been that easy? But it wasn't hard. Nothing had to be hard. I could see it now. Anything I wanted, I could reach out and get. I was not shackled in the ways humans were.

Riga surged forward. "What just happened? I saw a shimmer and then...you smiled. It frightened me."

I shook my head. "You should be frightened." I reached down into the satchel I had just pulled here from St. Louis. I grabbed the first object my hand touched and I clutched it to my chest. I looked down. It was a coin.

"Nice," I said. "Plumeria's lucky coin. I'm sure she's hiding away somewhere." I reached in again. This time it was a pink rock that even I recognized. A drop of Forlorn blood. Marveaux's blood.

"Two trinkets might be enough," I said though they weren't my words. "The coin's practically worthless, but Plumeria wasn't one of our best and brightest, now, was she?"

17

"Plumeria?" asked Mink. If I didn't know better, she sounded faint, as if she were afraid or surprised.

I grinned. Mink and Plumeria had been at each other's throats even before the war. Both envious of the other's beauty, both beautiful beyond the ability of a human language to describe. Mink's wings gentle lilac, Plumeria's wings in a multitude of dusky pinks. Together, they were a beautiful sunset.

True, Plumeria wasn't as clever as Mink, certainly not as strong-willed. Mink could torture Brooklyn for hours to get what she wanted, whereas Plumeria would merely snap the human's neck with her long, delicate fingers. She wouldn't realize there could be a point in acquiring information before killing.

Mink visibly pulled herself together from the surprise of hearing her old rival's name. "Get on with it," she said. "Get this thing open. Your friend's life is on the line."

A deep anger rose from somewhere deep in my soul. Mink was overstepping every boundary she had once abided by. I remembered the way she'd looked at me, looked at my lovers Soul's Anguish and Lightbearer, the way she thought she'd buried her envy and jealousy where I could not see.

But I had seen. Mink was a pitiful member of our race. And yet, I had done my best to save her, just as I had desperately tried to save the others.

I shook my head. Where were those thoughts coming from? I did my best to push them aside, but they sat in my brain, heavy and solid, completely unmovable.

Brooklyn moaned one more time and slumped to the ground. It might be too late; fear now squeezed itself into the anger. The anger didn't leave, but it slid to the periphery, allowing the fear to enter and grab onto my organs, to make my stomach twist, to make cold sweat break out up and down my spine.

I held out the coin in one hand, the pink crystal in the other. I thought hard about the hole in the universe before me. The sinkhole. A pocket universe forged from the fabric of the universe itself and sewn into a pinched-off not-place that the creator could use to store things. The creator, but also me.

I could control it. The fear wouldn't help with that, but I couldn't banish it. No matter how much I ignored it or attempted to push it aside, the fear slid around my defenses and gripped my soul ever tighter.

Fine. Leave it be.

I clutched the coin and the crystal and imagined the hole in the universe before me opening. The entrance was closed tightly, and the boost of energy I got from the items I held wasn't great. Not surprising; neither Marveaux nor Plumeria were terribly gifted. Opinionated, beautiful, loyal to themselves above all. They had that in common. But the power their tokens held was still valuable. I would just have to focus harder.

The thoughts that were not mine kept coming and it was difficult to differentiate between what I thought and what someone else was thinking in my head. I was sure I'd never heard of Plumeria before. I'd had no idea what color Mink's wings had been. The thoughts running through my thoughts could only belong to one person.

The pretentious bitch who was dead, and yet still retained a great power, as if she'd never died at all.

I wanted to scream, to drive her out of my head. But her thoughts and mine melded in an alarming way I had no control over.

My hands squeezed the relics and a power rose in my chest. It was hot like the sun yet did not burn me to ash. Alternately, it was cold, and it froze my heart as if to keep it from beating.

No, there was no *as if* to it. My heart stopped.

Simultaneously, a wave of red-hot power shot out from my skin. Instantly, the sky clouded over, and the sea began crashing into the shore. Swimmers and beach-walkers shrieked and ran up the beach, grabbing towels and leaving beach chairs and umbrellas behind.

In contrast with the heat, which poured out from my skin as if a dam had broken, the ice in my chest that kept my heart from beating seeped out, slow and deadly. It coiled onto the sand in front of me. It hesitated briefly, and then, without any fanfare, the sinkhole opened.

Beyond the sand at my feet I saw legions of Rakes, rows upon rows of scraps, shadow people whose form remained vaguely human, but twisted as if somehow in terrible agony. Beyond them were crazy folklore creatures like flying lions, human-headed birds, fire-breathing worms, and hybrid animals like half-scorpion, half-human men. The combination was hard to look at, as if my brain would not, *could not*, truly understand their chimeric dimensions.

Beyond that were objects that seemed to be exploding stars caught in the act of expansion, voids so black my eyes refused to even rest on them, and the glittering ruby droplets of millions of gallons of blood. Forlorn blood. Some of it had faded to a dull pink like the crystal in my hand. The rest was crimson and velvety black as if freshly shed. A bloodbath had happened, not recently, but somewhere in the ancient past, and the spilled blood remained here, wet and sticky. And utterly disturbing.

But that was not the end of the colorful yet disturbing vistas; as I watched, one last layer swam into view. Beyond that, beyond the seas of blood, at the very depths of the sinkhole, stood the one whose absence had been a hole in my heart for thousands of years.

Soul's Anguish. He stood stiffly, as if bound by chains. His white face was tilted upward so that his long ink-black hair flowed down his back like a shining dark river. His eyes were closed. He stood like a statue, as if he had been here mere moments and was merely resting for a brief respite before continuing whatever activity had been interrupted by this quiet moment of stillness.

How well I remembered his wings, so black they were nearly invisible in the vastness of space. The black had been relieved only by a small white mark on the leading edge of each feather. He had always been the one with the deepest emotions, the one who grasped everything he loved and refused to let go. If he loved something or someone, he wished to control them. He could not face life without their return love shining on him like starlight falling upon a black hole. The black hole consumed it, and was enlarged, but those in its vicinity inevitably faded away as their very essence was consumed one dainty kiss at a time.

Except for me. His passion could not drain me. His love could not change me. The Lightbearer and I were the only two who were proof against Isya's power of draining the very substance of anything his heart desired. That was his nature; he could not arrest it, nor put it aside. It was as intrinsic to him as his all-encompassing love.

"Isya," I said. My voice contained all the pent-up love, admiration, and despair I had kept inside for so long. I had missed him. Longed for him. Had found it easier to die and turn away from eternal life because I couldn't face eternities without him.

His eyes opened. The void-dark irises were so dark they could not be told from the pupils. He smiled. "Zireya. I have dreamed of you."

I could not smile in return. His absence had been too painful, my death too heartbreaking, to feel any joy at this moment. I felt only relief at the moment. Relief that even one of my loves was here with me.

"I have mourned you," I said. "Your loss was too much for me. I died. I have been in a sinkhole as a shadow of my former self for much of the time we've been apart."

His expression darkened. "Then the Lightbearer has been the Lord of All in my absence."

That did get a bitter laugh from me. "Hardly. He mourns in his own way. Except for a few compatriots, he is generally alone."

"Serves him right," Isya said with a look of distaste. "He trapped me here. I need to find him and get my vengeance."

"I thought you might feel like that," I said. "And the thought grieves me. I had not thought to release you just yet, but Sweet Song at the Edge of the Vastness forced my hand."

He shook his head. "She could never force you."

I tried to get my thoughts back, and then, just for a moment, grief overwhelmed the other's mind and the alien thoughts retreated. I grabbed my chance. The world around me—the sand, the wind, the angry sky—were once again real and I welcomed the sensation of being in control of my body once more. "That's cause she's fighting me, you asshole. Stay in the pit. We don't need a war of eternal beings happening on our planet."

Isya's expression hardened, as if the angles and planes of his true form were aching to get through the line of his jaw, the edge of his cheekbones. As if his human form could not contain the ancient form we had abandoned so long ago and his emotions alone might force a change back. "Who are *you*?"

But the other was too strong. and my control faded as quickly as it had come. "Just the mortal I'm using to speak to you. My body is elsewhere, and it has been empty a long time."

His face cleared. He looked around and then nodded slowly. "I can leave here," he said at last. "The barrier is gone."

"I handled it. Even now, trapped in death and requiring this mortal form to speak to you, none of you are a match for me."

"None of us were *ever* a match for you." He shrugged his shoulders, cocked his head, and in an instant, he was gone.

No doubt he was in search of the Lightbearer. Ware had better watch his back.

I turned around. The other mortal, the one Mink threatened, was still on the sand, now soaked by the driving rain coming down from the purple sky. Mink stood in the rain almost within touching distance, while Riga had retreated a few feet. The older woman rapidly blinked rain out of her eyes.

"That's it?" asked Mink. She stared at me. "He's out?"

"Yes, Sweet Song," I said. "Now you will let the human go."

Mink physically flinched at the nickname. "Of course, my Queen." She backed away from Brooklyn, who began gasping for air. She would be fine.

"Queen? You threatened me," I said. "Do you think that's acceptable?"

Mink dropped to her knees and bowed her head. "I didn't know I was speaking with you, my Queen. I didn't realize..."

"But it's what you hoped. The mortal could never have opened the sinkhole."

Mink hesitated. She almost glanced up; I could see the movement begin in the muscles of her neck. But she thought better of it and her head remained bowed. "I didn't know. I thought perhaps you might be aware enough to hear, to affect her actions. Or I thought, if she feared for her friend's safety, she would be able to tap into a power she didn't know she had. I didn't know you were aware enough to take her mind from her."

I turned my back on Mink and reached my mind for her. I could absorb her essence as I had the Tunneller. But here, beyond the world of the sinkhole, I could not drain her life force. I frowned. This mortal form had weaknesses I had not truly realized.

"Go. Do not let me see for you a long time." When next we met, I would be ready. Mink was mine, had always been mine, and would be mine as I drained her of will, power, and life.

But for now, she was free to go. I could reclaim her at any moment. She knew it. I knew it. No one needed to say it out loud.

Mink whimpered. "Yes, my Queen."

I spared no more thought for her as she slithered away.

Another was in the area, though. He was more powerful than Mink but, still, not powerful enough to get in my way. But if I could not drain her now, I certainly could not drain him. Not yet. That would have to wait until I became more familiar with this new form, these new physical rules.

"Musician," I said.

He did not approach; I felt his presence nearby. He had hoped not to be noticed.

"We have no business at present," I said. "Go where you will. I will call you in time."

In an instant, he fled. That left me alone on the beach with the remaining two humans. Everyone else had fled to shelter due to the rain and waves I had called. I allowed them to recede. I had the power, but channeling it through this mortal was tiring, and strange to me. I would have to go slow, build my knowledge and abilities. I would adapt, and evolve and become what I needed to become.

Brooklyn remained on the sand, eyes closed, breathing heavily. I turned from her to look at the old woman. Riga.

Hands trembling, she reached into her purse. "You did it," she said, voice filled with loathing. "You let him go. You've brought a war to Earth that none of us will survive."

"You won't," I said. "Go ahead, take that weapon out of your purse."

She blinked in surprise. Did she think I hadn't noticed?

"You want to shoot me," I said. "Would that make you feel better? Would it bring your husband back? Would it make the world right?"

"No," she said with a sneer. "But it would help." She pulled out the gun and held it awkwardly, pointing it in my direction.

"That won't do," I said. I waved in her direction, a languid movement that distracted me briefly. This human form was so much more supple than the crystalline body I had worn for so long.

I caught myself before the human could realize my inattention. I looked back at Riga. "You'll point that at yourself. Kill yourself."

The woman kept the weapon pointed at me. "No. You're the one who needs to die."

"I have been dead longer than you know," I said. "I am far beyond your comprehension."

I stared at the human woman, willing her to obey. My will was powerful, but I hadn't used it in some time. Not like I'd used it today. Even so, the woman surprised me by her ability to resist.

Seconds passed, and while she did not shoot herself, she did not manage to pull the trigger while the gun was pointed at me, either. She trembled, and she tired.

I kept my will on her. Pressing. Pushing. Forcing her, eventually, to turn that muzzle toward her own head. Her eyes were afraid, her mouth open in horror.

The sound of the gun was muffled by a crash of thunder and the muzzle flash was covered by the lightning that streaked through the sky overhead at the same moment.

Satisfied, I watched her body collapse to the sand. But I knew that would not be the end of it. I had sensed it. She was one of the special ones, the foot soldiers in the coming war.

Her form appeared to grow jelly-like, then paled. Her hair slid off her body, her features collapsed. Slowly, she transformed into something useful. Long-limbed, tireless, full of rage and hunger. A Rake.

The thing stood and sniffed, wanting to feed.

"Never mind that," I said. "Go into the sinkhole. Wait for me there."

The thing had no choice, despite its hunger. It hissed and threw itself into the sinkhole. I closed the thing and sent it back to the Midwest. Back to St. Louis. I needed to go there next, to face *him*. To see the Lightbearer. To decide if he were still of use to me or not.

But that was to come. Now I could relax. I did not need to ride this human all the time. It was tiring, trying to move with this weak body, trying to speak with this oddly-shaped throat. Let the human have her body back. For now.

The woman on the beach opened her eyes. The horror in them was amusing.

"I'll see you again, I'm sure," I said. "For now, farewell."

I retreated. Time to rest and plan.

18

Brooklyn and I got off the plane in St. Louis two days after the fight on the beach at Pass-a-Grille. Two days of nightmares. Zireya might have retreated for the moment, but she'd left me with the memories. I could barely sleep when my mind's eye kept replaying Riga's death. Her murder. The bitch queen hadn't cared a bit for the woman, had no compassion whatsoever. And she'd slid into my mind and taken over without a hint that it had even been hard for her.

I had briefly thought I should pick up the gun and point it at myself, but I knew she would prevent me from harming myself. She needed me, at least for now. I wouldn't be allowed to do anything that would harm the human she needed to ride.

Brooklyn held my hand as we walked toward baggage claim. After two days of caring for an unsleeping woman who kept moaning about watching Riga die and turn into a Rake, she was well aware of the thoughts I couldn't banish.

"Don't worry," she said, for probably the ten thousandth time. Sometimes I could hear tears in her voice, at other times, she had more control and sounded supportive, even though we both knew there was truly nothing she could do. "We'll figure something out. We will."

I think she was trying to convince herself, because she wasn't convincing me. Whatever was going to happen next, it would not be anything I chose. My fate had been handed over to this ancient being who had more power than I could ever hope to understand, and who had more iron will than one human could withstand.

"Sure," I said. "We'll figure something out."

"And if we don't," said Brooklyn, "we'll go out fighting."

That actually made me smile. "Absolutely. We'll go out on our terms, not hers."

Brooklyn nodded and squeezed my hand, then dropped it to grab our luggage. It was time to go home.

About the Author

Marella Sands is a native St. Louisan who has published novels, novellas, short stories, a poem, an essay, and non-fiction works. Her historical novels, *Sky Knife* and *Serpent and Storm*, were set in 5th century Central America. In addition, she co-wrote two King's Quest novels with fellow St. Louisan Mark Sumner under the name Kenyon Morr. She has had short stories in several anthologies, most recently in *Merciless Mermaids*, edited by Kevin J. Anderson. She has always been interested in cemeteries, sits on the board of one, and also is a volunteer at Cahokia Mounds State Historic Site in Collinsville, Illinois (horseradish capital of the world and home of the world's largest ketchup bottle!). She and her husband travel whenever they can and stop by old cemeteries when they have the opportunity.

Marella earned degrees in anthropology from the University of Tulsa and Kent State University. The author's household includes the author, her husband, and a multitude of pets.

Contact Me!

Have you come into contact with the paranormal? Would you want to tell your story? I am currently researching a series which will feature UFOs, Bigfoot, shadow people, angels, demons, Ouija boards, and ghosts, among other things. I need personal stories to integrate into the series. You can be anonymous, or be identified by first name only, if that's your preference. If you're interested, you can access a submission form by using this QR code.